GUN FOR SALE

Lee E. Wells

GUNSMOKE

First published in the UK by Hodder and Stoughton

This hardback edition 2012
by AudioGO Ltd
by arrangement with
Golden West Literary Agency

ISBN 978 1 445 88146 1

British Library Cataloguing in Publication Data available.

Printed and bound in Great Britain by
MPG Books Group Limited

Lee E(dwin) Wells was born in Indianapolis, Indiana, the foster son of Robert E. and Nellie Frances Wells. He attended school in Indianapolis and later, in California, studied accounting and became a licensed public accountant and the owner of his own business. With "Pistol Policy" in *Western Aces* (4/41) Wells began publishing Western fiction in the pulp magazine market. As early as "King of Utah" in *The Rio Kid Western* (Winter, 1943), Wells began contributing feature novelettes for Western hero pulps, including feature novelettes for *Range Riders Western*, *The Masked Rider Western* along with more Rio Kid adventures. Authors could take personal credit for these stories as opposed to some hero pulp magazines where writers were forced to work under a house name, such as Wells's Jim Hatfield novelette "Gold for the Dead" in *Texas Rangers* (2/47) as by Jackson Cole. *Tonto Riley* (Rinehart, 1950) was Lee E. Wells first hard cover Western novel. This was followed by such outstanding Rinehart titles as *Spanish Range* (1951) and *Day Of The Outlaw* (1955). The latter was notably filmed as *Day Of The Outlaw* (United Artists, 1959) starring Robert Ryan, Burl Ives, and Tina Louise. Wells learned later in life that his birth name was Richard Poole, and he adopted this as his pseudonym for a number of impressive novels such as *The Peacemaker* (Ballantine, 1954), filmed as *The Peacemaker* (United Artists, 1956), and the outstanding *Danger Valley* (Doubleday, 1968). Whether as Lee E. Wells or Richard Poole, his Western fiction is noted for his wide and vivid assortment of interesting characters and the sense of place and people he could create within his imaginative ranching communities.

I

CLAY MANNING had been traveling the high country, moving with the careless persistence of one who knows where he is going but has no particular time to get there. He was like a man released from jail in this wild area of jumbled peaks and magnificent distances.

Narrow streets whose yellow dust always seemed to hold the seeds of violence and sudden death, false front stores, squalid saloons, the garish hell-holes of the red-light districts held no meaning up here, yet these things had been a daily portion two months past. And perhaps the memories of daily patrols, his hand near his gun, the gleaming badge on his shirt a perpetual target for the gunslinger avid for a reputation—maybe these would fade, too. After ten years as marshal of one of the most lurid "end of trail" towns, Clay Manning wanted to forget it all.

He no longer had to hunt a man—or be hunted. He no longer had to kill—or be killed. Yet he had gained his release in a swift burst of gunfire and had a fresh scar along his ribs and a belt full of money to show for it. Joe Blakely, train and bank robber, had chosen bullets rather than the hangnoose; Joe Blakely had died before Clay's gun. In dying, he had given Clay Manning nearly thirty thousand dollars in various rewards.

Clay knew that now he had his one chance to change a dream into a reality—buy a ranch of his choice in the country of his choice, settle down and become a man of substance rather than a half-feared gundog for the law. Not that this was something to be ashamed of. He had tamed at least one small section

7

of the primitive West and his successor could carry on. Clay had heard tales of the Morala Valley country, up beyond the mountains that he now threaded. It was supposedly rich in graze, well-watered; the paradise a cattleman never expects to see in this world but wistfully hopes he will encounter in the next.

So here was Clay Manning with the money around his waist, as he rode into Chieftan, the county seat of Morala Valley. He had dropped down out of the high country, made his slow, observant way through the grazing land of which he had heard so much. Rich, deep grass covered this great valley surrounded by mountains. The valley was not flat, but rolling, with here and there a few small hills. Ranch country—dream country—and he could not deny it, but he looked for the flaw he felt must inevitably appear.

Perhaps Chieftan was that flaw. Clay wondered why men could not have built the town to blend with the distant, majestic peaks that lifted jagged fingers against a clear-washed sky. He passed the livery stable and corral, the blacksmith shop, dirty and sooty. There was the general store, three saloons, the squat millinery shop, the Bon Ton Department Store, a café, the Elite Hotel before which Clay drew rein. The arrangement was different but the false fronts and boastful names were all the same.

With a slight lift of hope, he noticed that no railroad tracks bisected the town, but at the far end of the street he glimpsed a couple of small shacks with a furtive, secretive look. He could guess who lived there. A few side streets led off this main one with a scattering of houses—some average cottages, a few more pretentious.

Clay swung out of the saddle and strode up the steps to the hotel porch. Two old men, sunning themselves, eyed him with silent curiosity. Clay gave them a brief nod and went into the lobby.

A few cracked leather chairs lined one wall, with drooping rubber plants at either end. A short counter stood before a board of keys and a rack of pigeon-holes. A thin, balding man adjusted his glasses and

8

peered near-sightedly at Clay. He looked mildly surprised that someone had walked in.

"Room?" Clay asked.

"Room? Oh, sure—got a nice room." In a fluster, the man shoved a register toward Clay. "Staying long?"

"A day or two, a week, maybe longer." Clay shoved his dusty hat back from coal-black hair. As he bent to the register, his tanned face and slightly hooked nose gave him an Indian cast.

The man turned the register about. "Clay Manning . . . Kansas," he read aloud. His mild, brown eyes widened behind the glasses. "Clay Manning! You the sheriff?"

"That's right. At least, I was—"

"Clay Manning! We've heard plenty about you up here!"

"Thanks. Now if I can—"

"Say, some business bring you up to Chieftan?" A faint edge touched Clay's patient drawl. "Business of my own."

"Sure! Sure!" the clerk said hastily. "Say, our sheriff would sure like to see you. Jake Toller would be mighty pleased to shake hands with Clay Manning."

Clay leaned on the counter, blue eyes level. "Can Jake Toller wait until Clay Manning gets a room, a bath and something to eat?"

Alone at last in a room overlooking the street, Clay looked around. The bed was a brass frame with a pancake of a mattress and a paper-thin blankets. There was a battered washstand holding a big china bowl and a huge pitcher with a cracked lip. The flowered wallpaper held oily stains. Only the cheerful light from the two windows overlooking the street gave warmth to the room. Clay shrugged, turned to pour water from the pitcher into the bowl.

When he went downstairs again, the clerk directed him to the Chieftan Café, across the street, next to the sheriff's office.

Clay found the Chieftan to be ordinary in furnishings but a cut above the average in food. When he went out on the street again, the sun had gone down

9

behind the western ranges so that only the sky was still bright. There was a stilled, blue quality to the air and the buildings seemed taller and softer in the peculiar light. Sounds were strangely muted, peaceful.

His eyes caught the sign of the Concho Saloon and he decided to pay it a visit. In the easy friendliness of a saloon, a man could learn much about the country.

He heard his name called. He turned, saw a portly figure standing in the door of the sheriff's office. "Ain't you Clay Manning?" The man stepped out on the walk, hand outstretched. "I never figured I'd have the pleasure of meeting the best damn lawman in the West."

Clay saw the star pinned on the beefy chest. He smiled and shook hands. "You'd be Jake Toller."

"That's right—Sheriff of Morala County." Jake considered Clay, looking up into his face. He smacked his lips. "Say, this calls for a drink, Manning—one lawman to another."

"I was just going to the Concho, Sheriff."

Toller swung in beside Clay and they crossed the street. Toller was around forty, Clay judged—five years or more older than Clay. He had a round face, made moonlike by fat jowls and a nose that had been flattened over thick lips in some far-off time. His eyes were a watery green. The rounded paunch, the tracery of veins about the nose suggested Jake Toller had more than a passing knowledge of the bottle.

Clay had met other lawmen of Jake's obvious caliber—men good enough to handle the law in an out-of-the-way county but who wouldn't have lived through the first day in the trail towns. Courageous, probably, but a little slow in thinking, fatally slow in a gun draw.

Toller was affable. He bought two drinks and would have bought a third, but Clay refused. Jake pursed his lips, disappointed. "Why, man, you ain't wearing the star!"

"That's right." Clay covered his glass as Jake still tried to pour another drink. "Habit, I guess."

Jake nodded. "I know how that can be." He looked

10

then at Randall and Kristan as the three men lined up before him. Wariness showed in his eyes.

"Clay," he said, "I hope you ain't going to make a fuss over that Tumbling A rider. Once things are peaceful, leave 'em that way."

Clay quickly checked Randall's angry move. "We don't know yet, Jake. Depends on you."

"Me?" Jake caught himself. "Now I can't go after that man when there's witnesses say he shot in self-defense and—"

Clay leaned over the desk. "Jake, we think we have a way to bring peace to Morala Valley. I want to go to Tumbling A. I want to speak direct to Lora Archer—and alone."

"Talk to her! About what?"

"Our side of the story, something the sheriff should have done long ago." Jake's heavy jowls flushed as Clay went on.

He searched Clay's face, then the others, back to Clay. He scratched his chin. "How you going to talk to her?"

"First thing in the morning, you ride to Tumbling A. Tell Miss Archer we want peace. Tell her there's two sides to every story and it's fair that she listens to ours. I'll talk to her."

Jake still considered. "I could do that," he said doubtfully.

"Tell her that I'll come alone and I'll wear no guns. I won't, and can't, cause trouble. We'll talk it over. Is that fair enough?"

Jake moistened his lips. "Sounds right to me."

"Then you'll ride out and prepare the way?"

Jake's face cleared. "I'll do it. Like you say, it's a chance for real peace." His face fell. "But suppose she won't listen?"

"I think she will," Clay's face hardened. "If she doesn't, then the rest of us know exactly where she stands."

XII

LATE THE NEXT DAY, Jake Toller rode into the ranch-yard and Clay went out to meet him.

"Saw her," the sheriff said. "She didn't want to at first but finally she come around. Tomorrow, you'll get your talk."

"Thanks, Jake," Clay smiled. "You've done the Valley a service."

Jake lifted the reins. "I ain't sure it'll get anywhere. Her mind's already made up."

"I figured that, for now. But let's see what happens."

"Sure," Jake reined about and spoke over his shoulder. "Good luck, Clay. Sure hope you have it."

The next morning at breakfast, Lew Mahler looked out the window and said, "We got company."

Clay went out on the porch. Kristan and Randall dismounted and came up on the porch with a nod for Lew. Randall sniffed the air. "Sure smells like coffee."

"Come in and sit," Clay said.

Over the coffee, Randall explained the reason for their presence. "Jake spread word Tumbling A will talk to you, Clay. We figure you need some backing. So Larry and me will ride with you."

Clay placed his cup on the table. "I said I'd ride alone." He glanced at their holstered guns. "And I said I'd carry no gun."

"We don't aim to wear these," Kristan said. "But three men look more like business than one, even if we don't say a word."

Clay shook his head. "No good. You heard the deal

I made with Jake and Miss Archer agreed. I stick with it."

In disgruntled silence they helped him and Lew straighten up the kitchen but they exchanged glances now and then. They waited in the ranchyard while Clay saddled up. When he rode out, they swung into saddle.

Clay drew up. "Now where you going?"

"With you," Randall said, "as far as the Tumbling A line. No harm in that, is there?"

"No point, either."

"Maybe. I wouldn't put it past Latigo Dolan to bushwhack you so you wouldn't get a chance to tell the truth." He glanced at the gunbelt around Clay's waist. "Maybe you figured the same thing, wearing that hardware."

Clay capitulated for the moment. "Come on."

They rode in silence until they came to the line of low hills, threaded through them and stopped. Beyond lay Tumbling A and there was no sign of a rider. Clay unbuckled his gunbelt and hung it on the saddlehorn. He took the gun from the holster and put it in a saddlebag, strapped it down.

He looked at his companions. "This is as far as you go."

Kristan frowned. "Blake and me will ride wide—way off to one side. Won't be too far then if you need help."

Clay shook his head. "Alone. I don't want any chance of Lora Archer backing out. So you stay here."

He smiled grimly, and rode forward. Kristan and Randall sat their horses, watching him, a tall, straight figure. At last he dropped down into a swale and disappeared from their sight.

Clay rode steadily on. His eyes constantly sought the horizon for some sign that he was watched even now. He did not completely rule out the idea of a trap but thought it unlikely. Tumbling A knew only too well that if he didn't show up again, they had a range war on their hands.

He came to a ranch road that cut across the range to join the main road. Clay turned into it. The headquarters could not be much further. Clay rode on, trying to shape what he would say to Lora Archer.

Suddenly four men rode out of the trees. They turned to face Clay and waited. His hands tightened on the reins but he did not check his pace. The man in black could be none other than Latigo Dolan. The other three were part of the Tumbling A crew.

Within a few feet, he drew rein. The three riders watched Clay, and Latigo Dolan's thin lips twisted in a sardonic grin.

He straightened. "This is as far as you go, Manning."

Clay's blue eyes held him. "Are those Miss Archer's orders, or your own idea?"

"Who's to say?" Latigo answered carelessly. "Point is you turn back here."

"I have something to say to Miss Archer," Clay said evenly. "She's agreed to see me."

"There's been a change. Speak your piece to me and I'll pass it on to Lora. We like it better this way."

Clay's jaw hardened. The three men with Latigo eased their horses forward so that they pressed about him, one so close to Clay's right that his foot touched Clay's stirrup. Clay indicated his gunbelt hanging on the saddlehorn, the empty holster. "I've kept my word. Miss Archer told Jake she'd see me. That's the way it stands."

"Manning, you don't savvy. You're stopping here. You keep arguing and you might stay here with a bullet in your hide."

Clay's eyes grew steely. "Miss Archer didn't send you, Dolan. She keeps her word. So you came out here yourself."

Latigo shrugged. "Like I said, it doesn't matter."

"Afraid the truth will reach Miss Archer, Dolan? What did you tell her about the Box E raid? Who pushes her toward gunsmoke?"

Latigo jerked erect, dark face tight. Clay continued, his voice even. "Does she want to avenge her father? Was she told he made a gunplay, and died—or that he was murdered? Who gains by telling her these things?"

Latigo's black eyes blazed and his hand dropped to

106

his gun, half drew it and then he let it drop back in the holster. "Now it'd be a shame to shoot down a man who had no gun. But I remember when you first showed up in the Valley."

Clay's eyes darted to the man beside him who affected two guns, and then back to Latigo as the *segundo* chuckled. "Seems like some of the boys who worked on you the night of the dance weren't hard enough. Only laid you up for a short spell."

Latigo's eyes cut to the men, savoring his next order. Clay took this split second when Latigo held the men's attention. In a swift fluid motion, he snatched the rider's gun from the holster, swung it up. Clay lined the muzzle on the *segundo*'s black shirt. He dogged the hammer back, held it ready to fall.

His calm voice checked the move of the men for their guns. "Don't try it! Tell 'em, Dolan. Any little thing can make this hammer drop. You'll die the next second."

They froze. Latigo's hand was on his own weapon but his black eyes held in fascinated horror on the gun hammer strained against thumb and spring, ready to drop. The black muzzle held steadily on his chest. Latigo spoke tightly. "Not yet, boys."

"Tell the boys to ride ahead," Clay instructed. Latigo hesitated. "Go on, tell 'em! Any reason why I shouldn't kill you after what you've pulled?"

Latigo studied him, less in fear than a weighing of chances. He saw there was none. "Ride ahead," he said.

"Toward headquarters," Clay amended. "I'll be right behind you and this Colt will be aimed at your back. You'd be sorry if something went wrong. Let's get on."

Latigo gave him a venomous look and wheeled the horse about. The three gundogs rode ahead of him, now and then throwing a helpless look over their shoulders. Clay followed Latigo, gun never wavering from the man's back.

They finally rode into the huge Tumbling A ranch-yard, a strange procession. The road led directly up to the ranch-house and, beyond, Clay saw the spread of the pens, corrals and buildings. There's enough here for any man, he thought fleetingly. Why had Dan Archer wanted more?

As they approached the house, the door opened and Lora Archer came to the porch. They were still at some distance but Clay saw the angry set of the slender shoulders.

They were close to the porch when Clay spoke evenly. "That's far enough."

Lora stood tall and straight at the rail, an angry goddess, green eyes flashing fire. Her full lips set in disdain as she looked at the gun in Clay's hand. Her voice was like the fleshbiting flick of a lash. "So this is the way you keep your word! Unarmed! You're a born liar like all the rest of them."

Clay held his anger down. He indicated the rider with the empty holster. "This is his gun."

He pitched the weapon to the man, who caught it, held it poised, and then shoved it in the holster, stealing a glance at Lora. His act had told the whole story. Her lips parted slightly, then closed again.

Clay swung out of the saddle, lifted the bags from the horse and carried them to the edge of the porch. He held them up to Lora, and indicated his own gunbelt. "Empty, Miss Archer. You'll find my Colt in one of those bags, strapped down. These men met me on the road. Mr. Dolan didn't want me to see you. Tumbling A has broken its word, not me."

Lora looked hard at her foreman. "Is this true, Latigo?"

"I figured there was no point in bothering you—"

"That will be all, Latigo," she cut in coldly. "I told Mr. Manning that I would talk to him. Get to the bunkhouse. I'll call you when I need you."

Latigo's furious eyes held Clay's a moment and then he neck-reined the horse and headed around the house. The three men followed, avoiding Lora's angry face.

She turned to Clay. Her voice was softer but the anger lines did not leave her lips. "Come in, Mr. Manning."

Without waiting for him, she swept inside. Clay

crossed the porch and entered through the open doorway. He took off his hat and eased the door shut behind him. His glance covered the big room, rested on Lora who stood tall and unbending by a table. Her voice choked a little.

"I must—apologize for my men, Mr. Manning. I knew nothing of it. I excuse it only because Latigo is over-zealous for the ranch—and my feelings."

Clay inclined his head but said nothing. He waited until Lora made an impatient gesture toward one of the chairs. "Please be seated, Mr. Manning."

He took the chair. Lora moved to another, sat down, shoulders straight and stiff, hands folded in her lap. Her beautiful face seemed carved from granite and she cut sharp each word.

"Sheriff Toller can be a persuasive man." Acid came in her tone. "Especially if he feels he might have to work for the star on his shirt. So I agreed to this talk, Mr. Manning."

Clay smiled. "I thought you'd be fair."

Her lips softened, then tightened again. "I shall make myself very clear. I'm willing to listen to what you have to say. Sheriff Toller hinted that I had only a part of the story—that there was another side."

"There always is," Clay cut in softly.

Her eyes flashed. "I doubt it. I knew my father very well—we were always close. I knew what he faced. He told me time and again. I know that your people killed him. So I am prepared to listen to lies, Mr. Manning —old lies that started before my father died. It is fair that you know what I feel."

Clay caught his upper lip in his teeth as he looked at the floor, gathering his thoughts. He had not expected her to be so open and blatant about her preconceived opinions. If he argued the point, he might only make it worse.

"You've read a clear and open brand, Miss Archer," he said slowly. "So I'll tell you exactly where I stand. I don't go along with what all people think about Tumbling A—or you."

"I'm glad to hear it," she said but there was sarcasm in her voice. "However, you did grab land my father wanted. You've fought Latigo. Just the other day you accused one of my men of deliberate murder. Your words, Mr. Manning, and your actions don't ride the same trail."

He made a slow count to keep from blurting a hot retort. He continued to speak carefully. "Ma'am, a lot has happened on both sides of the fence. A lot of it happened because no one ever sat down and talked like you and me are doing right now."

She sensed his implication. Her fingers tightened in her lap. "Go on, Mr. Manning."

"I got to talk about myself, ma'am, for a minute. I heard about Morala Valley down in Kansas. I came up here, not knowing anyone, not knowing all that had gone before. I wanted to buy a small spread. I didn't have enough money to make a mistake. So I looked around and I talked to folks."

"And you joined the wolves—" she stated, but Clay's lifted hand cut her short.

"We can argue that out later, ma'am. I learned one thing for sure and I can tell it to you square and honest. The folks around you—your neighbors—want to live in peace with Tumbling A. They don't want an inch of range they haven't come by honestly through buying it or filing homestead where it's been declared government range."

"A lie, sir! My father once owned all Morala!"

"Owned, ma'am? or settled her and claimed it?" Before she could protest, he continued, speaking quickly but with no heat. She let him go on, though he could not tell from her expression if he made his points.

He reviewed all that he knew of the early days when Dan Archer first came. He brought it down to the present time, telling it the way he had heard it. Now and then she started to protest but always caught herself, letting him continue uninterrupted.

Clay took a deep breath. "That's the way folks see it up until what happened at Box E. I was there right after, ma'am. I heard what Mrs. Epps had to say, and the hired hand. I saw sign. I do believe those folks."

He then recited the attack on the Box E as he was certain it happened. Her face grew bleak and once he

110

thought she would cry. But her pride rescued her and her eyes flashed again. Now and then he could sense protest, but she allowed him to continue. At last he finished.

Lora Archer sat unmoving, the sea-green eyes looking at a great distance out the window. Then, slowly, her lips curled. "You are saying that Latigo lied to me. You are saying that my father, a kind and just man, tried to drive another off his rightful range and was killed. You are saying my father intended to kill first."

Clay looked at her quietly. "Maybe there's better ways of putting it. You got to judge for yourself. Ask Latigo and the crew and see if their stories tie in. But you ought to ask folks who talked to me, too."

"It would be a waste of time. Latigo and the men are loyal—they would not try to fool me. I know what my father was like and, because of that, I know what you have been told is a lie—whether you believe it or not."

She arose and Clay came hastily to his feet, knowing that he had lost. She spoke coldly. "Perhaps you tell the truth as you see it. But they have lied to you also. My father was murdered."

Clay made a last, desperate gamble. "Look, Miss Archer, say you're right and your neighbors are wrong. Peace can still last in Morala Valley. Clean the slate as of now—all the past. Your neighbors will leave you alone. You can live with them."

"That asks for a lot!" she exclaimed angrily.

"Maybe. But hate and fear of Tumbling A will be gone. It has been built up. Things done in the past by both sides can end here and now."

"You're again saying my father was a range hog!" she snapped.

"I'm saying he made mistakes—bad ones. I'm saying you don't have to make the same mistakes, like forcing folks to sell ranches or be driven out—letting gunmen loose on ranch and town."

Her face grew vivid with fury. "I'll not listen to this about my father! He took land that once belonged to him."

"He'd never taken title," Clay started.

111

She cut in, "You talk for those land-robbers. Why, you're even their gundog, brought in by them. Father knew that."

"Then he was wrong!" Clay said hotly. "Like he was wrong about a lot of things!"

"Get out, Mr. Manning." She strode to the door and whirled to face him. "And get out of Morala. I'm warning you."

Clay straightened. They glared at one another, tall man and tall girl. Clay's blue eyes narrowed and he spoke quietly, yet his words were harsh. "You've made a bad mistake just now, Miss Archer. I don't hire my gun to anyone, for any price. Nor am I driven off by anyone, even if that person's a beautiful, stubborn pig-headed woman!"

She gasped, eyes wide. Red flamed up her neck and into her cheeks. Her lips changed to a thin line and she moved so swiftly that Clay was taken by surprise. Her open palm struck his cheek a hard blow, the sound of it flat and sharp. It rocked his head.

Anger riding him, he instinctively grabbed her and then he did something that surprised even himself. He pulled her to him and held her close as he kissed her. Her fists beat futilely at his sides and back. She strained away from him.

Then, suddenly, her lips grew soft under his and the steel went out of her body. She was surrender and delight for a second. Then she realized what she did. Her elbows and arms forced him away and she broke loose.

Her red hair was disarrayed and her eyes full of fire as she whirled by him to a marble-top table against the far wall. She jerked open the drawer and lifted a Colt, swung around to face Clay, the black muzzle lining on him.

"Get out!" she spat, "before I kill you! Don't ever come here again. Tell that to your friends. Tell them I'll have them shot if I find them on Tumbling A range —or in my way."

Clay took a deep breath. He looked at the gun in her hand then up at her. He picked up his hat from the floor where he had dropped it, faced her again.

"I shouldn't have—done that. I lost my head."

"Get out—before I shoot you."

His lower lip protruded as he studied her. Her body shook with gusts of anger. He nodded. "I'll get out, Miss Archer. But remember, you can have peace —or war on this range. It's peace if you listen to your own reason—war if you listen to others. Tumbling A's next move will show what you've decided. For your sake, mine—everyone's—I hope you figure things right."

The gun muzzle lifted in a menacing reminder. Clay looked at it and his lips moved in a crooked smile. He met her angry eyes, his own dancing. "As for killing me—you won't."

He deliberately turned his back on the threatening gun and walked out the door. He heard her angry gasp.

XIII

CLAY STARTED across the porch, glimpsed Latigo squatting on his heels under the shade of a tree several yards distant. Clay heard the quick rush of feet behind him as he descended the steps, strode to his horse.

Lora's voice lifted sharply behind him. "Latigo!"

Clay swung into the saddle and faced the porch. Lora stood at the head of the steps, the gun still in her hand at her side. One arm was raised, the small fist clenched against her chest.

Latigo came striding toward them. He kept his right hand near his gun, his black eyes sharp and hard on Clay. Clay studied Lora, lean face calm.

"Better think things over, ma'am," he said quietly.

Latigo halted a few feet away, arm crooked so that his hand hovered over his gun butt. His voice was sharp. "Anything wrong, Lora?"

She took a deep breath and dropped her arm. "I—no, Latigo. Mr. Manning's leaving. I want to—talk to you. Right away."

Latigo frowned, his glance darting from her to Clay, back to Lora. He sensed something had happened and that Lora held a seething anger in check under a surface calm.

Clay touched his fingertips to his hat. "I'll tell your neighbors that at least you'd listen."

He wheeled the horse around, his gaze sweeping over Latigo who stared back, his frown deeper. Clay rode slowly away, his powerful back solid and square to the girl on the porch and the man in the yard.

Latigo stood watching Clay. He looked at Lora over his shoulder. "Sure nothing happened?"

"Sure," she said shortly.

"You're holding Dan's gun," Latigo said. "He try anything?"

She shook her head, pulled the gun back so that the folds of her skirt hid it. "No, I got the gun when he— first came in. I didn't fully trust him." She turned to the door, wondering at her own evasiveness.

Latigo gave Clay's receding figure a last, weighing look and then he shrugged, turned to the house. Lora was gone now and Latigo moved slowly up the steps, his frown deepening.

He pushed open the door without knocking and stepped in just as Lora turned from the table where she had replaced the gun. She avoided his probing glance for a moment and then met his eyes almost defiantly.

Latigo pursed his lips. "All right, what happened?"

She walked to the window, looked out on the yard a moment and then sat down on the sofa. "We talked— or rather I let him talk. A couple of times we both got angry."

"That's why the gun?"

"That's why," she said and Latigo noticed the slight flush that came to her cheeks. She hastened on. "He believes what he told me, Latigo, but he had it all twisted and changed around."

Latigo sat down beside her. "Twisted how?"

She told him, repeating Clay's version of her father's actions. Latigo did not interrupt, but his dark features reflected his scorn of the story.

"It makes Father sound like an—an outlaw, Latigo!" she exclaimed. "How could they believe this of so fine a man!"

"They don't," he said flatly. "That's just a cover." He took her hand. "They tried to steal Dan blind. So they tell these stories to make their side look right."

She nodded. Suddenly she launched into Clay's version of the attack on the Box E. She spoke tightly, her voice strained, but her eyes never left Latigo's face. She read nothing there, even his eyes seemed veiled.

"Is that true?" she asked when she finished. "Manning said that he was at the ranch soon after."

Latigo looked at her, accusingly. "Lora, if you believe his story, then you sure didn't know Dan very well. He was a hard man, he had to be. He was fair, though."

He repeated in detail the story he had first told her. She listened for any discrepancy and, far back in her mind, wondered why she did. This had to be the truth. Her father could not have deliberately tried to kill a man and be shot down himself in the attempt. If so, then everything else said about him could easily be true. But she knew better! He was a grumpy old softy. He stood up for his rights but he took from no man.

Latigo finished. Actually, his story was much like Clay's—all the events were there in both stories. But she could see how Clay had turned things here, put a false implication there, had Dan drawing first instead of Jory Epps, as it should have been.

Her full lips curled as she thought of Clay. "Liar!" she said aloud.

Latigo nodded. "A troublemaker, nothing more." He took her hand again and his voice softened. "Lora, you waste time talking to people like that. It gets us nowhere."

She nodded, suddenly weary. "I know. But I couldn't let them say that I wouldn't talk to them—at least once."

"So you did talk—and it ends where it started. Remember, you and me once planned what we would do? It's time we went ahead, Lora. If we don't hit first, they'll hit us."

She said nothing. Latigo pressed the argument. "Dan would have done it that way. If the hired gundog, Clay Manning, is driven out, we'll have won half the fight. The rest will make a wide swing around us."

He waited. Lora remembered all too vividly Clay Manning standing over there by the door. He had said that Tumbling A's actions would prove its desire for peace or war. There was the definite implication that Manning and his friends would fight back.

She wanted nothing like that if she could avoid it.

116

But she would face gunsmoke if Tumbling A was attacked. Let the wolves make the first raid. Latigo waited her reply and there was an eager light in his face.

She hesitated a second longer. "Not yet, Latigo— not quiet yet." He started to protest but she pushed on. "We'll keep within the law. If anyone pushes, we'll push back—and harder. But wait until someone pushes."

"But Dan wanted to get back all of the old Tumbling A!"

"We will," she said firmly. "But we'll buy out. Money can do as much as guns, and easier. We try that way first."

"But they won't let you live in peace," he insisted.

Her jaw hardened. "If they won't, then we'll cut loose the guns. But not until we're pushed, Latigo."

He shrugged and looked disconsolately down at the floor. Another thought struck him and he gave her a covert, measuring look. She studied the tips of her shoes, her thoughts far away.

Latigo's eyes narrowed and he moistened his lips. "Lora, there's something else."

She started. "Yes?"

He spoke carefully. "It's about us, Lora."

She looked at him in surprise and he smiled, the hard angles of his face strangely softening. This sudden warmth made him a truly handsome man.

"Dan used to talk a lot," he said, "about what he planned and what he hoped. Time and again he said he wanted you to marry well and he hoped it would be a man he would like. He wanted to be at your wedding —" his voice drifted off. "I hope this ain't the wrong time to bring this up. But you need to know you have someone right at your side you can depend on. Me, Lora."

"Latigo, I—"

"Something else you should know," he hurried on. "I reckon I fell in love with you the first day I come to Tumbling A."

She said nothing, only looked at him. Latigo leaned toward her. "I just want you to know, Lora. It's no time for a wedding now, but maybe in a year you'll consider marrying me?"

She was momentarily taken off balance. Everything was in Latigo's favor, and yet. . . . She made a confused little gesture. "I—don't know, Latigo. There are so many other problems that I—it's not the time to think of it."

His eyes darkened and his smile became a little fixed. He expelled his breath in a soft sigh. "Maybe you're right," he conceded, "but you will think on it?"

"Of course, Latigo!" Now she put her hand on his, gave it a little pressure. "I am flattered—honored. But, later?"

"Sure." He stood up and smiled down at her. "Work to be done. I'll see you this evening."

He left, closing the door softly behind him, walked to the top of the steps and stood there, hands shoved in his hip pockets, his dark eyes looking out to the distant hills.

All Tumbling A range—as far as he could see. And southward spread more range that could eventually be brought under rule of Tumbling A as Dan had planned. Latigo's thin lips moved in a sardonic grin— as he had encouraged Dan. Now the old man was gone, and with him the plan.

Latigo's brows arched—maybe not. Part of the plan had been marriage to Lora, the breath-taking, beautiful girl in the room behind him. It would still come— give it time. Then all she had would be his. Then he could push out again, and in time Latigo Dolan would be the ruler of a kingdom—all of Morala Valley. It was a big shining golden dream and close to reality.

He descended the steps and turned toward the corral. His voice lifted with a new confidence as he spoke to the men, setting them to work.

Clay Manning headed back to the spot where he had left Kristan and Randall. He slouched in the saddle, thinking of the meeting with Lora Archer and made a wry grimace. What could he say for it? He had gained little or nothing.

He was certain that Lora Archer had never known

118

the truth about her father. It was apparent in her speech, in her belief that old Dan had been kind and gentle, a fair man under a crusty exterior.

She believed that Jory Epps had deliberately killed her father—she made murder of it. That meant that Latigo Dolan also kept the truth from her. Clay couldn't fight a dead man and maybe it was best for Lora to have this high opinion of her father.

But Latigo Dolan? He was the real menace to the peace of Morala Valley. Clay understood the man, gained from his experience in the trail towns. Latigo exactly fitted the pattern of the driving, ambitious man. He would not long take orders from Lora Archer and he already pushed her in the direction Dan had taken.

Maybe Latigo planned to marry her. The thought disturbed Clay and he hoped it would never come about. He returned to the main problem. He hoped that Lora would cross-examine Latigo and the crew about the fight at the Box E. Some of them would be bound to make conflicting statements, slips of the tongue. Lora would begin to have doubts about her *segundo*. Doubts would make her look back and she might come to see events in their true light. If that happened, then Latigo's hold on her would be broken. Her innate fairnesss—and Clay still firmly believed in it—would bring about some means of peaceful living between Tumbling A and its neighbors. Maybe in this way, the talk with Lora had been worthwhile.

Suddenly he saw Lora Archer as she faced him with the gun in her hand. He vividly saw the flashing emerald-green eyes, the golden-red hair, one lock disarrayed. What a beautiful woman! Uncontrolled, his thoughts recreated the few brief seconds when she had been in his arms, her soft, supple body bent against his. He tasted the brief surrender of her lips. Rouse that proud girl and she was a woman of fire! He shook himself loose from the swirling thoughts. A crazy, useless thing to be thinking about. She was not for him—ever. That kiss and that embrace was the last he would ever have.

He touched spurs to the horse and sped along the trail, blanking his mind to thoughts of Lora Archer.

119

Blake Randall and Larry Kristan waited where Clay had left them. They sat under the shade of a tree, but hastily stood up as Clay came in sight, faces eager, eyes questioning. They stepped forward when he reined in and dismounted.

Larry smiled, his eyes showing his relief. "What happened? Did you get anywhere?"

Clay shrugged. "I don't know." He took the gunbelt from the saddlehorn and strapped it around his waist, then took out his Colt, and slid it into the holster.

Randall blurted, "Tell us, man!"

Clay recounted what had happened, omitting only that Lora had pulled a gun on him—and the kiss. Both men listened, Kristan frowning now and then. Randall's face mirrored his disappointment. Clay finished and Kristan sighed deeply.

"Sure don't sound like much."

Randall flung his arms wide. "Nothing gained at all! Our troubles have just started. You'll see."

"If she questions Latigo— "Clay began.

"She won't," Randall said with flat finality.

"I'm not sure," Clay insisted.

Randall looked sharply at Clay. "You ain't thinking. By God, I think she's got a hex on you. You're under the spell of that witch."

Again Clay felt the remembered pressure of her lips.

"She is a witch—but a pretty one." He smiled. "But her spell's not very strong, Blake."

He turned to remount as Blake exchanged a puzzled look with Larry Kristan.

XIV

CLAY RODE into Chieftan with Randall and Kristan and told of his meeting with Lora Archer. As Clay expected, it caused divided opinions, but he had done what he could.

Clay returned to his ranch and threw himself into the work. There was much to be done and, besides, he wanted to forget the memory of a kiss, a supple body. So long as he guarded his thoughts, he could push the picture away. But it would come back at unexpected moments.

Now and then neighbors would drop by, Randall or Ole Neff. From all of these people, Clay had news of the Valley. Tumbling A kept to itself except for one visit to Chieftan. There had been no trouble. Clay decided his visit to Lora had had some effect. At least the continuing peace made Clay believe that she had decided on peace.

Lew Mahler surprised him around noon one day toward the end of the week. He came into the barn where Clay worked and jerked his thumb over his shoulder toward the house.

"She says come in and eat," he said laconically.

"She!" Clay exclaimed and jerked around. "Who!"

"Mrs. Epps. Did you expect Lora Archer?" Lew asked with a grin.

Clay flushed for thought of the girl had flashed through his mind. He frowned at Lew. "When did she get here?"

"About an hour ago. Went right into the kitchen.

Said us men need a decent meal. She wouldn't let me tell you she was here."

Clay went out with Lew to the washbench and then into the kitchen. Diane turned from the table where she had just placed a bowl of steaming vegetables. She posed prettily in the light from the window, the soft gray dress giving her the air of a schoolgirl. Her warm smile flashed teasingly at him.

"Surprised?"

"Mightily," he replied. She caught his puzzled look.

"I'd been to town and when I came to your road, I wondered if there wasn't some way to show thanks for all you've done for me. I thought a meal would be just the thing. There it is."

"But you didn't have to—"

"I wanted to, Clay Manning! Sit down—and eat!"

She was a cook, no doubt of it. Clay and Lew finally eased back, replete and Clay looked at his empty plate. "I can't stir up a meal anywhere near like that one."

"It takes a woman's touch," Diane laughed easily. "Now you boys help me clean up the dishes before you get back to work. I have to be getting home myself."

The dishes were quickly washed and put away, the kitchen straightened. The work done, Lew walked to the door and grinned at Clay. "Reckon work won't wait. I leave you to see the lady off. I sure thank you, Mrs. Epps."

She laughed and dismissed his thanks. He bobbed his head and was gone. Diane smoothed her dress, looked up at Clay. "I'd best get along. My buckboard's hitched out front. Lew said you couldn't see it from the bar." She laughed at his rueful grin. "It was a surprise, wasn't it?"

"A fine one. Haven't had a meal like that in a long time."

Her eyes sobered, though her smile remained. "You need a woman around here." She added quickly, "I've yet to meet a bachelor who wouldn't be better off."

He grinned. "Kind of depends on who's talking, don't it?"

"I guess it does." She turned quickly to the door. "Have to be getting along."

He felt the sudden constraint between them. They walked in silence to the buckboard and she gave him a brief smile when he offered his hand to help her up. He stepped back as she gathered the reins.

She studied him gravely. "Would you count a woman 'bold' who speaks her mind?"

"Why, no. A woman has a right to speak."

"I'm going to talk up, then. I don't think one thing has been very clear. I'm in love with you. You should know it." She smiled wryly at his stunned look. "I *am* bold. But it can help you make up your mind."

She waited but Clay could not find words to speak. Shadows came in her eyes and her lips set, then broke in a smile again. "Well, come visit the Box E, Clay. I promise you I won't be forward again."

She lightly slapped the reins and the buckboard rattled out of the yard. Clay remained looking after her. He had sensed the note of shame under the mocking gaiety of her invitation. No woman should feel that. It was his fault that he had not responded to open honesty. Why in hell, he wondered, couldn't he just marry her and combine the two spreads? What held him back? a nebulous, half-formed dream of someone else?

He turned away with a feeling of anger at himself.

At the same moment, on the Tumbling A, Latigo Dolan came out on the porch of the ranchhouse, Lora at his side. They had been discussing ranch problems. At the edge of the steps, Latigo looked at the girl, his dark eyes softening.

"Something else I want to remind you about."

"What?"

"Me . . . you and me. Just to keep you thinking of it."

Her face clouded before she smiled and shook her head. "Not now, Latigo. Not now."

"When?" he pressed.

"I don't know. Soon, I guess."

He studied her, saw the wisdom of retreat. He laughed. "All right, that's fair enough."

He touched his finger to his hat brim and jauntily descended the steps, headed for the bunkhouse. The crew saw him coming. Lora remained on the porch as the men gathered about Latigo.

She could see he gave crisp, direct orders, and she noticed the alacrity with which the men moved. Latigo turned to the foreman's cottage. Lora stood thoughtful, tapering fingers lightly touching the porch rail. She looked up to the jagged lift of the mountains against the sky and seemed to try to read something there. Then, with a sigh, she turned back in the house.

Latigo entered his cottage and pitched his hat on a sofa. He strode across the room, spurs jingling loudly, and took a bottle and glass from a small cabinet under a mirror. He poured a sparing drink, stared down into its amber color for a moment and then, with a shrug, tossed it off.

The gesture made him aware of his reflection in the mirror. He placed the empty glass on the table without taking his eyes from his own image. He inspected himself carefully. What the hell was wrong with him? A lot of men were worse looking. He was no stranger to Lora Archer and her father had considered him a top man, dependable.

What then? He didn't know. Damn it! Lora knew that Dan wanted her to marry him. Dan had made no secret of the letter he had written and placed with his will. Lora must have read it.

Latigo went to one of the windows, looked musingly out on the yard. He saw Lora turn slowly back to the house. His black eyes narrowed and his lips pursed and twisted thoughtfully. She kept putting him off. There was a shadow of reason to some of her excuses, like the correct period of mourning, but why had she not warmed up to him?

There was a change in Lora Latigo didn't understand. At first she had been filled with hate of those who had killed her father—a faint smile touched the corner of his lips. He had thought then that she would strike once the first rush of grief was over. Instead, she spoke of buying out the spreads.

Being a woman, Latigo had rather expected a first, peaceful approach to fulfilling her father's dream. But nothing had happened. Worse, Lora didn't seem to

124

care. She perked up only occasionally, as when that fool, Chris, had killed his man in Chieftan. She'd stood up then, ready to fight. Then, once they were home she had told Latigo to let the man go—one of the best gunslingers on the payroll. Undependable, a trouble-maker, she had said, and all of his arguments had not changed her mind.

Now Clay Manning had come and once more she had revived. Because of Clay? He scoffed at that idea. But whatever Clay had said was beginning to work with Lora. She seemed to have forgotten her father's dream.

Latigo looked toward the bunkhouse. Inactivity was making the crew grow restless. Always a fiddlefoot lot, they wouldn't be content to sit in the sun and scratch much longer. Something had to be done to hold them. Something had to be done to counteract whatever Manning had told Lora about the small ranchers. She had only mentioned briefly that Manning had "told their side." Later she had hinted that their side might have a certain amount of reason.

That line of thought had to be stopped, and quick. It would take Tumbling A to do it, for Latigo knew that Manning held the small ranchers in check. He frowned, everything had started to slide from the time Manning came into Morala Valley.

Latigo swiped his hands over his thin lips. Maybe the war could be started without her. Latigo poured another drink, walked back to the window. His eyes circled the horizon, picturing the positions of the various spreads around the Tumbling A.

Box E? With Epps dead, that sexy wife of his would be alone except for a hand or two. Better leave it alone until Latigo could be certain the woman would not be there. No point in her getting accidentally shot. Manning? Latigo tossed down the drink with a savage gesture.

If he were knocked out, a lot of starch would go out of the rest of them. Manning didn't want war, but Manning would be a rallying point for the rest once real trouble started.

Latigo slowly worked the empty shot glass around

in his fingers as he considered the other spreads. Suddenly the glass stopped moving. Ole Neff's place! Small —out of the way. Ole wouldn't put up much of a fight, if any. The boys could see to it there wouldn't be much left of the ranch.

It would be warning to the Valley—it would start things moving. If it was followed by another swift, hard attack, Tumbling A could grab range fast before the small ranchers could get their breaths.

Latigo hurried out the door. He went to the corral, saddled up, headed out of the yard. He found the men he wanted a few miles away, cutting hay and showing they didn't like the job.

There were five of them, and Latigo pulled them into a squatting group under the shade of a tree. Their disinterest left after his first words and their ugly eyes gleamed. Latigo marked out the position of the Neffs' Lazy N and gave his orders. They listened avidly and then one of them stood up.

"When?"

Latigo grinned. "Nothing gained by waiting. Take the rake in. Get what you need and ride off—to the south. Circle east and head directly for Neff's. Remember, if Miss Archer ever asks, you were line riding."

One man gave Latigo a querulous look. "Then this ain't her idea?"

Latigo shrugged. "She's talked about it, but she can't work up enough nerve to give the orders."

"And you know what she wants," the man said. His grin grew meaningful. "I reckon, the times you spend with her, you ought to, huh? Well, I'm damned tired of cutting hay."

The group went back to their horses and the rake. Latigo watched them go and then with a pleased smile, turned to his own mount. He swung into saddle and rode leisurely back to the ranch.

Near sundown the next afternoon, as Clay and Lew started to the house to prepare supper they saw the rider streak into the yard. They hurried to meet the man, sensing that something of importance had happened. It was Tom Duggan, one of Blake Randall's hands.

"Meeting tonight at Blake's," he said, reining the horse in.

"What's up?" Clay asked.

"Hell's broke loose," Duggan answered laconically. "Ole Neff and his hand is dead. Their beef has been run off."

"My God!" Clay exclaimed. "Who?"

"Figures Tumbling A. Blake and Larry Kristan are calling folks in this part of the Valley together. I got to get on to Box E."

He rode off, heading toward Box E. Lew spoke softly, "Looks like your friend kind of ripped things apart."

"Yes," Clay said slowly, "but I wonder." He turned on his heel. "Let's get supper and head to Blake's."

The small main room of Randall's house was crowded when Clay and Lew entered. Clay nodded to his neighbors and then saw Diane Epps, seated near Blake.

Randall acted as spokesman and chairman. He told Clay what had happened, so far as they were able to reconstruct it. Five or six riders had hit Lazy N and there had been a hell of a fight. Ole and his brother had been killed.

"Happened yesterday afternoon or last night," Randall said, "near as we can read the sign. Cleaned 'em out. Kristan sent for Jake Toller and some of us went with him." Randall's face worked angrily. "There ain't nothing left but the land and buildings. Jake picked up the trail and followed it into the mountains. He lost it up in that broken country."

"Then there's no proof who did it," Clay said slowly.

"Real proof—none," Randall agreed, and the others stirred restlessly. "But I reckon all of us know who's behind it."

Clay found a spot against the wall while the rest talked excitedly. There was actually little information, mostly guesses. Clay sensed the direction of the meeting, the mounting fear and tension against Tumbling A; it was serious, all right.

Blake Randall finally summed it up. "I figure we

can't get anywhere with talk. There's no point in walking soft for fear we'll start a war. Tumbling A has done it. We'd better band together here and now and we'd better let Lora Archer know we're not to be picked off one by one."

"I'm for banding together," Clay said slowly. "I agree that the raid on the Neffs wasn't rustlers—even though we couldn't prove that in court. That's why we have to move slow."

"And let them get us!" a man burst out.

Clay held up his hand. "Figure it out. Nothing in this ties in with Tumbling A. Suppose we make a wrong move? Tumbling A already owns the sheriff. If they struck back, it would be in self-defense—they'd claim." He paused. "And I just can't believe Lora Archer would order deliberate murder."

Diane Epps stirred and all eyes turned to her. Her voice was calm but Clay saw anger gleam far back in her eyes. "Clay, you lean over backward. After what happened to my husband, the gun fight in Chieftan, and now the Neffs, I think it's time we quit splitting hairs. Maybe Miss Archer didn't order this but it was her men who done it. So, she's to blame. I say let's stick together. If we don't, the Tumbling A will get us one by one."

Discussion surged up and Clay briefly answered questions put to him. Back in his mind, however, was the prodding hunch that this attack on the Neffs was completely out of character. He could not tie it in with Lora as he knew her, brief as that had been.

He listened to the talk and finally said, "Whatever you do, you can count me in."

It mollified Randall and the others.

They decided they must have some system by which anyone attacked by Tumbling A could get immediate word to his neighbors. They would then give a warning to Lora Archer that she could attack at her own risk. Tumbling A would keep, within bounds, on the range and within the town. They decided to hold a meeting at Kristan's within three days. With this, the group broke up.

Diane Epps worked her way through the crowd to Clay. "Mad at me?" she asked.

He grinned. "Not very."

"Good." She walked through the door with him. The yard was dark. Men spoke to them as Diane, linking her arm in Clay's, led him toward her own buggy. "I came over with Duggan. Hank's holding down the ranch."

"You shouldn't be alone," Clay said sharply.

She smiled. "Afraid your friend will bushwhack me?" Her fingers made an instant pressure on his arm. "Maybe that wasn't fair, Clay. But you keep defending her so that—well, sometimes, a person would almost think you were in love with her. Are you?"

"Of course not!" he blurted and then wondered. "I tried to say that this could be Latigo Dolan's work—not hers."

"And he's her foreman," Diane reminded.

"I know." He was silent a moment. "I'm just trying to make sure we don't make a bad mistake."

They were at her buggy. She pressed his arm again and he helped her climb to her seat. She leaned toward him. "I'm glad that's the reason, Clay." Her smile flashed out. "Now take me home. It's a long dark way and—I like a strong man along at times like these."

He stepped back and she slapped the reins, the horse taking off at a sharp trot. With a grin, he realized she forced him to come along. He took long, swift strides to his own horse, climbed in the saddle and turned it in the direction Diane had taken. He rode at a slow trot.

They were right, he thought, he *had* leaned over backward. Old law training, maybe, or the memory of a kiss. He shoved the thought away. He had settled that with himself.

He heard the rattle of Diane's buggy ahead. Why did he hold back? He didn't know, but he felt now that it had been foolish. He spurred the horse and sped ahead. The shadow of the buggy loomed up close in the road.

129

XV

WHEN HE PULLED up beside the buggy, Diane called without halting the pace, "Thank you, kind sir."

He laughed. "My pleasure, ma'am."

They rode on for several miles, the only sound the dull thud of hoofs in the thick dust, the rattle of the buggy wheels, the creak of Clay's saddle. Suddenly Diane drew rein and Clay asked if something was wrong.

"Yes, I need a driver."

He swung out of saddle, tied his horse to the rear of the buggy and climbed into the seat, Diane making room. He picked up the reins, clucked to the horse and they rolled on. He threw her a glance out of the corner of his eye. She faced him and her laugh was soft.

"I said I was bold, Clay."

He drew rein, put out his hands, drew her to him. She came willingly and her body and lips were clinging. At last they slowly drew apart, Clay shaken by the impact of her kiss.

"We'd better get on," Diane said in a muffled voice. "You make a woman lose her head, Clay."

He picked up the reins and the buggy rolled on. His thoughts whirled like dust devils. He finally broke the silence. "Diane, we've had time to think things over."

"I know what I want. Do you?"

"I reckon I do."

Her hand touched his arm in a caress. "Then it's settled. As soon as a decent time has passed."

"Sure."

She caught some of his confused thoughts. "Clay,

you thinking about Jory?" Before he could answer she spoke with understanding. "Sometimes I do, too. But he wouldn't mind, Clay. I lived up to my bargain fair and square. I never looked at another man except once —at you. And that would've come to nothing had he lived. I can tell you that."

"I believe you," he said.

"Now Jory's gone and I've got a lot of years ahead —we've got them. Jory would understand."

They were silent again. They came out on a high meadow and Clay swept the dark, star-studded horizon, a habitual thing. His eyes passed by and beyond the faint glow and it was a second or two before his mind registered. His eyes jerked back as he sharply halted the buggy.

"What is it, Clay?" Diane asked.

He leaned forward. The faint glow was there and grew stronger, pulsing now. He pointed and Diane now leaned forward, too. Her head turned and she stared at Clay.

"Is it—fire?"

The glow grew stronger, more definite. His jaw set. "At my place—or yours. Can't tell at this distance. Can you bring the buggy?"

She nodded. He jumped out and swiftly snapped his mount's reins loose from the buggy. He jumped in the saddle, came up alongside and leaned down to Diane.

"Head for my place first. If it's all right, then yours. Be careful."

She nodded. He set spurs and was off. Diane pulled the whip from the socket and lashed the horse. She guided the careening buggy with deft, firm hands down the dark road. The sound of Clay's horse drummed away into the distance ahead.

Clay raked spurs and the horse responded. The wind whipped his face as he raced along. He came to his own ranch and found it dark and peaceful but now he could see the angry red against the sky further along. Box E.

He jumped out of saddle and raced to the house. He groped his way through the dark to the bedroom Lew

131

Mahler occupied. As he approached the door, Lew's sharp voice sang out. "Who's there. Stand hitched. You're under a gun."

"It's me. Get dressed, Lew. Fire at the Box E. Diane's coming along in the buggy. She'll need help."

A match flared as Lew cursed. It took him but minutes to dress and then he was out of the house, racing to get his horse. Clay looked at the red glow against the sky, then hastily turned back into the house. He grabbed rifle and scabbard, dropped ammunition for it and his Colt in his pockets and hurried out to his horse.

Lew came up. "That fire an accident, you figure?"

"Don't know," Clay said quickly. "I keep thinking of the Neffs."

Clay led the way out of the yard at a dead run, Lew's horse pounding behind him. They had a brief glimpse of Diane's buggy but Clay didn't stop. She could see for herself the location of the fire.

The dark miles sped by. Lew said nothing but grimly clung close to Clay's racing horse. Suddenly, Clay drew rein. Lew pulled to a sliding halt. Now that the drumming hoofs were silenced, they could hear a new sound. Gun fire—from the direction of the Box E. The two men exchanged glances and Clay set the spurs again. Lew followed.

Soon, even above the thunder of hoofs Clay could hear the sound of guns. He swept to the top of a low hummock that bounded the Box E yard and the whole ranch came into view. The barn burned fiercely, flames and sparks leaping high in the air, revealing ranch and bunkhouse. Clay saw gunflame spit from a window of the bunkhouse and then answering flames from the corner of the main building. He glimpsed two or three mounted men.

The attention of the raiders was concentrated on the bunkhouse, the burning barn. Clay saw a man fling a torch at another building. Clay slid the rifle from his scabbard and cut off at an angle, to come up behind the raiders. The crackle of flame, the roar of the guns, drowned the sounds of his approach. Lew trailed close

132

behind, freckled face grim as he pulled the Colt from the holster.

Clay made a quarter circle and dismounted, pitched the reins to Lew. He saw mounted men clearly lined in the flames.

He lifted the rifle, took a swift aim and the weapon gave a flat, harsh crack, bucked against his shoulder. One of the horsemen jerked erect, grabbed the saddle-horn. Clay levered another cartridge in the chamber as the raiders swung around. He fired again but his target moved at the last second and the bullet spat off into the night.

The raiders scattered, one of them grabbing the wounded man's horse by the bridle, leading it off. The single gun from the bunkhouse fired now in quick succession and there was an answering scatter of shots from the raiders.

They melted into the shadows but bullets sought out Clay. He jumped onto the horse and cut off at an angle, sliding the rifle into the scabbard and lifting his Colt from the holster. He fired as he moved and Lew's gun roared into the night. Clay hoped this would give the impression of many men, rather than two. Guns answered him, the bullets missing widely for the most part.

Then, beyond the house a careening shadow appeared, racing in from the road. Firelight caught it and Clay saw Diane's buggy, swaying wildly as it came into the yard. He yelled a warning, drowned beneath the noise. The horse had bolted and it raced straight for the blazing inferno of the barn.

Diane, half standing, vainly sawed on the reins. Clay set spurs just as the fire of the raiders turned on the buggy. The horse went down in a sliding heap. Diane threw her hands high and fell, thrown clear of the wreckage. She lay outlined by the flames, her dress moving slightly in the breeze that swept across the yard.

Clay forgot the raiders. He raced toward her. He was not aware that the guns had suddenly silenced and the only sound was that of the burning barn. He vaulted out of the saddle and ran the few steps to

Diane. He did not hear the sound of racing, fading hoofs.

As he bent over Diane, the bunkhouse door flew open and Hank Mears rushed out, gun still in his hand. Lew came in fast. Clay gently turned Diane over so that he could look at her face. Her eyes were closed and she breathed hoarsely. He became aware of a growing stain low in the chest.

Hank crouched beside him. "Is she all right?"

"Hit—maybe bad. We'll get her to the house."

He lifted her into his arms as carefully as he could and turned to the house. Hank raced ahead as Lew, Colt held ready, threw a searching glance at the darkness beyond the farthest reach of the firelight. The barn was gone, the flames beginning to die now. The raiders had fled.

Hank lit the lamp in Diane's bedroom. Clay gruffly ordered him to bring bandages and water. He looked with growing concern at her pale face and closed eyes. He gently turned her over to reach the hooks of her dress and he had them loosened when Hank came in with the water and bandages. Clay ordered him out and closed the door.

He worked Diane's arms out of the dress so that he could lower the top. He encountered chemise and, fearing the spreading stain, pulled a knife from his pocket and ripped the cloth down to the fair white skin, stained with blood.

The wound looked bad and Clay's blue eyes shadowed. He judged the bullet had struck the stomach or just above. He bathed and bandaged the wound to check at least the exterior bleeding. But she needed a doctor, without delay.

He eased her back on the bed and covered her with blankets, fearing the inevitable shock and reaction from the wound. He took a last look at the quiet, beautiful face, distinctly paler now.

He left the room, taking basin and bloody cloths with him. Hank and Lew sat in the kitchen, the lamp on, and now they both jumped up to face him.

"How is she?" Hank asked.

"Not good," Clay said. "I'm going for a doctor.

Hank, you and Lew stay here. Do what you can for her until I get back."

"She—she won't die?" Hank asked.

"I don't know. When did this happen, Hank?"

"About an hour before you come. I was stretched out on the bunk, dressed, figuring I'd put the horse and buggy away when she come home. Something woke me and I looked out the window. They were firing the barn. I'd turned out the lamp so I reckon they figured they had the place to themselves. I sure showed 'em different." He shook his head. "Barn was afire by then but I figured to get one or two—or at least keep 'em from burning anything else. Managed to hold 'em off until you come. It was close, though."

Clay nodded. "Who was it?"

"Looked like gunslammers to me. No need to guess much about this—after what happened at the Lazy N."

Clay, with a sick feeling, nodded. Tumbling A— starting to hit ranches one after the other. This was war and there could no longer be any hesitation. He pulled his hat brim low as he went to the door.

The ride to Chieftan seemed endless and black thoughts harried him all the way. He felt the tragic irony of the situation. After months of haunting him, Lora Archer had finally left his mind. In the buggy he and Diane had come close to an understanding and then. . . . He refused to think of it further.

He roused the doctor and then hurried to the livery stable to get a fresh horse. He had no time to spread the news but hurried back to the doctor's house to find the man ready to ride.

It was long after midnight when they finally rode into the Box E yard. The barn was now no more than a heap of glowing embers. The ranchhouse was dark but the moment Clay and the doctor rode in the yard, Lew Mahler sang out a challenge.

Only then did the lamp in the kitchen come on. Clay hurried the doctor into Diane's bedroom. It seemed as if she had not moved. The doctor dropped his black bag on the table and bent to her, pulling

135

back the blankets. He examined the wound and looked around at Clay, thin-lipped. "Better wait out in the kitchen."

"Will she live?" Clay blurted.

"Have I a crystal ball?" the doctor retorted. "It's bad—and that's all I know right now. Get out and let me get to work."

Lew and Hank had coffee waiting in the kitchen and Clay gratefully took a mug.

Now and then they heard stirrings in the bedroom, but the sounds always subsided and the doctor did not come out. Twice he yelled for water and white cloth for bandages. He broke the door briefly to accept them and then disappeared, firmly closing the heavy panels in their faces. They resumed the tense, yet dragging, watch.

Morning light revealed the great heap of smoking ashes that had once been the barn. At the far edge of the yard the dead horse made an ugly brown mound.

The doctor came out, red-eyed, rolling down his shirt sleeves. He came into the kitchen giving the three waiting men a brief glance. He poured a mug of the hot coffee, drank some and then nodded toward the bedroom door.

"I've done what I could. The stomach is punctured and the bullet ranged upward. I don't know if she'll live or not. It will be touch and go." He took another long drag on his coffee. "Who shot her?"

The three men exchanged glances and Clay spoke. "You might as well know. We figure it was a Tumbling A gunhawk. They raided the spread last night."

The doctor grunted, filled the coffee cup again. "I'll stay a while. Mrs. Epps will need someone with her all the time. Can you get a woman?"

Clay nodded. "I think so. . . . Larry Kristan's wife."

It was late morning by the time Clay returned with Mrs. Kristan to the Box E. The doctor reported that Diane seemed a little worse and he smiled wearily at the sudden concern in Clay's eyes. "It's to be expected. Point is, we still can't tell what'll happen, either way,

136

won't be for a time yet. You get out and keep yourself busy."

Clay found Lew and Hank in the yard. Tired as he was, Clay remounted and the three of them cast about for sign. It was not hard to find. They could plainly see the hoofmarks as the raiders came in on the ranch, from the east. Hank looked at the tracks and then in the direction from which they came.

"Wrong way for Tumbling A."

"Could have circled," Lew answered shortly.

Clay kept searching for further sign. At last he came on it. He saw a gleaming cartridge case, ejected by a rifle as the raiders had fired on the careening buggy when it came into the yard.

Then Lew, moving along side him suddenly spoke quietly. "Look."

Clay followed his pointing finger and saw the dull, rusty spots on the grass. He nodded. "We hit one of 'em. Can't tell how bad."

They moved on, faster now. The trail suddenly cut away as though leading out of the big ranch and, shortly thereafter, blotted out, scattering in all directions.

Clay drew rein, Hank and Lew on either side. Lew rubbed his hand wearily over hs freckled face. "How you read it, Clay?"

"The way you do." Clay's words were clipped. "They saw they had shot a woman and that scared 'em. So they headed for home. They saw they'd given themselves away. Then someone was smart and they tried to make anyone following them believe they headed for the mountains and scattered. They didn't. They went home—to the Tumbling A."

Lew nodded. Clay sat quite still, bleak, grim face turned toward the Tumbling A. He pictured Lora Archer as he had last seen her. His lips curled.

The Neffs killed and burned out. Raid on the Box E and Diane Epps hovering between life and death. How could Lora Archer give such orders? or allow Latigo Dolan to give them? Evil disguised as beauty, he thought. Blake Randall had rightly named her—witch. His fist doubled on the saddlehorn. No, worse than

137

that—fiend. Beautiful or not, she had some explaining to make to the law. Or, if she owned the law, then to her neighbors.

Clay turned his horse. He spoke with a tight, clipped voice. "I'm heading for Chieftan."

XVI

FIRST, HOWEVER, Clay cut back to the Box E. He arrived just as the doctor, red-eyed with weariness, prepared to leave. The man sighed when Clay asked about Diane.

"She's resting a little easier, but that means nothing right now. I have other patients and I need some rest. I think I can safely leave her for a few hours."

Clay hesitated a second. "Doc, will she live or die?"

The man passed his hands wearily over his eyes. "A doctor thinks in terms of life and preserving it. So he fights death wherever it threatens. He refuses to surrender."

Clay took the long ride into Chieftan, the doctor beside him. Twice Clay spoke of Diane, hoping that he could get some small ray of assurance, but the doctor had none to give. They came into the town and Clay pulled into the lined hitchrack of the Bravo. He dismounted, and men came out of the saloon door. Kristan shoved to the front of the group, as did Randall and they waited expectantly as Clay climbed up the steps.

"What about Mrs. Epps?" one of them asked.

"No change," Clay answered wearily. "Let's talk inside. I'm tired and I'd like a drink."

They made way for him. He walked to the bar and ordered.

"She's bad hit?" Randall asked.

Clay nodded. "She might live. She might not."

"Who did it?" a man in the crowd called.

Clay shook his head. "I want to talk that over with the sheriff first."

"Why? Jake won't stir his bones. We can handle it ourselves."

Clay straightened. Steel came into his tired voice. "Get this straight. We're not letting this raid go by. But we got law—"

"Jake Toller!" a voice called scathingly. "You call that law?"

He lifted his hands as protests arose. "We give Jake this last chance. I'd like for Blake Randall and Larry Kristan to go with me. We'll demand that he deputize us. If he won't take action, then we'll decide what to do. Do you agree?"

There was argument, but at last it was agreed that the three men would go to Jake Toller. They would return to the Bravo and report.

They found Jake in his office, sitting behind the desk as though it was a barricade. He smiled, but his eyes went to the door as though he expected to see a crowd outside. Clay saw the flood of relief in his eyes when he realized there were just three of them.

His voice grew a shade more confident. "Sit down, gents."

"No need," Randall snapped. "You heard what happened?"

Jake moistened his lips. "Heard talk. Nothing for sure and no complaints."

"You have them now," Clay said tightly. "Tumbling A hit Diane Epps' spread last night. The barn is burned. They shot Mrs. Epps."

Jake's hands clutched the chair arm.

"Shot her," Clay repeated. "She could die. Tumbling A has broken the law. You're the sheriff."

Jake stared, and took a deep, ragged breath; slowly he pushed himself back in the chair. "It's one thing to say Tumbling A—"

"And another to prove it?" Clay demanded. He smiled, a frosty move of the lips. "I was there when Diane Epps was shot. I traded bullets with the raiders."

"You saw 'em?" Jake asked.

"Not clear. But this morning I followed sign. It led east and then cut back over my range into Tumbling A. They broke up there, scattered. One man was wounded. I don't know how badly, but someone has a bullet hole in his hide he can't honestly account for."

Jake sat for a moment like a huge lump of clay, thick lip protruding. The three men waited. Finally Jake spoke without meeting their eyes. "I'll ride out to Tumbling A. Right away. I'll find out what I can and—"

"We go with you," Clay cut in quietly.

Alarm showed in Jake's face. "No!" He caught himself and tried to smile. "Now wait, Clay. This is something I can handle myself. No need to take deputies. I'll just ride out and talk to Miss Archer and Latigo."

Clay leaned on the desk, strong arms bracing him. He looked at Jake, his eyes level, hard, accusing. "Jake, once you said you and me were the same breed —lawmen. Now I'm beginning to wonder about you. I'm not the only one."

"Now wait—" Jake blustered and subsided.

"Something about Tumbling A has you boggered, Jake. It makes folks wonder—there's half the Morala Valley in the Bravo right now wondering. Are you afraid of Tumbling A? Or in their pay?"

"You can't say that! You can't prove it!"

Clay straightened. "You'll prove it, Jake. By what you do now. You'd better have witnesses—we three."

Their eyes locked and then Jake's slid aside. He looked toward the door as though he longed to be far away. He fumbled open the desk drawer and pulled out badges, dropped them on the desk. "All right. You're deputized." He gained a final shred of courage. "But I give the orders, understand?"

"You're the sheriff."

Jake had to go to the livery stable for his horse, so Clay, Randall and Kristan returned to the Bravo and the waiting men. Some looked incredulously at the badges.

Clay told them what was planned and many wanted to ride out with them. Clay objected. "Just us three— and Jake. If all of you go with us, it will look like a mob rather than a posse. Tumbling A could shoot before they'd know they face the law."

Clay walked out to the hitchrack. Randall and Kristan followed him and, after them, the men streamed out on the porch. Jake came up, drew rein. He cast sidelong glances at the porch as though he expected to be pulled off his horse. He spoke in a low, swift voice to Clay. "Let's ride. I don't want trouble."

"You don't have it—yet," Clay answered.

The four men rode northward. Behind them, the crowd watched.

Free of the town, Jake seemed to throw a weight off his shoulders. But, when he looked ahead toward the distant Tumbling A, his eyes shadowed. They came to the road leading to Tumbling A. Jake became increasingly nervous. Time and again he threw underbrow looks at his deputies as though he sought some means of dismissing them. Clay's feelings of contempt grew. Jake seemed to sense this, and was morose and distant.

They were well in to Tumbling A range when they saw riders approaching. Jake drew rein. Clay and the others pulling up beside him. The riders came on, fast, and in a moment Clay recognized the black outfit of the leader.

Jake spoke with quick apprehension. "Let me do the talking."

"You're the sheriff," Clay said.

Latigo gave a slight signal when the bunch was a few yards away and his men halted. Latigo came on, stopping before Jake. "I'm surprised at your company, Jake."

The sheriff made a mollifying gesture. "We want to talk to Miss Archer, Latigo."

"Why?" Dolan asked easily, but he was tense, ready.

Jake told him of the attack on the Box E and of the shooting of Diane Epps. Clay narrowly watched Latigo, caught the faint flicker of the black eyes from time to time.

"The trail led to this range," Jake finished. "This is mighty serious, Latigo. I have to look into it."

"Here?"

"The trail—" Jake started.

Latigo cut in, contemptuous. "Any horse can make a trail. No one here was at Box E. You can rattle your hocks back to town."

Jake's heavy jowls flushed and anger came in his eyes. "Now, Latigo, I'm sheriff."

"I said we had nothing to do with it," Latigo said sharply.

Jake's thick lips pressed and then his shoulders sagged. Clay leaned forward, facing Latigo. "This is law business, Dolan. It concerns Miss Archer. We're acting as a legal posse. Are you obstructing the law?"

Latigo made a faint smile. "Why, no. Just saving you time."

"Then let's see Miss Archer and account for all your hands."

Latigo's bold, scornful eyes rested on Jake, who didn't quite meet them, then on Randall and Kristan. His men became tense and waiting. Latigo faced Clay again and his hand dropped easily from the saddlehorn and hung loose, ready for a swift draw. He laughed and his eyes glittered. "You always talked big, Manning. So you demand to see Lora? Maybe you'd better start shooting your way in." His voice tightened. "Lora's not going to be bothered with half-baked lies. Get out, before I lose my patience!"

They sat frozen for a long moment. Jake made a queer, choking sound deep in his throat. He turned his horse and his voice was muffled. "Come on. No point arguing against that crew!"

"Wait," Latigo commanded, but never took his eyes from Clay. "You take my word for this, Jake?"

"Sure. Sure, I believe you. Why shouldn't I?"

Latigo smiled but his black eyes, boring at Clay, remained cold. "Just wanted it for the record, Jake. Now, ride off!"

Clay sat tall in the saddle, face set in hard and angry lines. Like Latigo, his right arm hung at his side but now his fingers slowly curled and a steely look came in his eyes.

Kristan forced himself between Clay and Latigo. "Clay," his voice held a sharp note of warning. "Not

143

now. There's too many of them. None of us are any good dead. There's another time."

The blinding anger left Clay. He gave a curt nod. "All right. Another time."

He turned, slowly, the action almost a challenge. Latigo made no move, simply watched. Jake Toller was already well ahead, walking his horse but still in flight for all that. Randall, his face showing a strange mixture of anger and prudence, swung in beside Clay and they followed after the sheriff.

Latigo's men started to move up but he waved them back with a quick, savage motion. Clay rode with his eyes fixed on Jake's broad back. He fought down an impulse to turn around, have it out. But Kristan was right—the odds were too great.

They rode back to town without speaking. The three made no attempt to move up beside Jake, and the sheriff felt their dislike and withdrawal. Nor did he much care. Jake Toller faced the ruin of his own self-respect. So they came into Chieftan. Men waited at the Bravo. Jake gave them a scant lowering glance and started to ride on.

Clay broke the silence. "Better turn in, Jake."

"It ain't my office," Jake growled.

"Still afraid?"

Jake glared at Clay and turned in to the rack. They went into the saloon, crowded as before, and Jake headed immediately for the bar. He busied himself with the bottle and a much-needed drink. After he had downed it he stood staring at the empty shot glass.

"Come on! Wht happened?" someone demanded.

Jake faced the crowd with a false bravado bolstered by the glow of the whisky. "We went out to Tumbling A. Talked to Latigo Dolan. He said no one on the spread was at Box E."

There was a long silence. Then a voice lifted in amazement. "Is that all? You *asked* Latigo Dolan. You didn't look for yourself?"

Clay cut in. "Just four of us. We faced a bunch of the Tumbling A crew—ready for trouble."

Jake pushed away from the bar. He searched Clay's

face, looked away. "Thanks, Clay. I'm going to my office."

He walked out and no one stopped him. The batwings closed behind him. Then angry talk burst like a torrent.

A man stepped forward. "So what do we do? We can't let Tumbling A get away with this! They'll shoot and burn all they damn please!"

Another spoke up with an angry shout. "There's enough of us here! I'm for going out there!"

"Wait a minute!" Kristan stopped them. "I agree we got to act—and fast. But I won't stand for any vigilantes. We go out there, we go to bring in those who shot Mrs. Epps for a fair and square trial." He turned to Clay. "You're used to law work. You lead us—keep things in hand."

Clay hesitated. But he knew these men would go, with or without him, and realized they needed someone who would check any lynching. He spoke slowly. "I'll lead you. Saddle up and wait for me. Larry, you and Blake come along."

Randall and Kristan swung in behind him as he walked out the door. The crowd flowed out into the street, heading for their horses. Clay walked toward the sheriff's office.

"You still going to waste time with him?" Randall asked.

"This is necessary."

Clay said no more. They entered the sheriff's office and Jake turned from his desk. "Can't you leave me alone? I rode with you."

Clay looked at Randall and Kristan. "You be witnesses." He faced Jake. "Sheriff, the citizens are going out to Tumbling A. They want you to go with them."

"A useless thing!" Jake exclaimed in frightened exasperation. "We have Dolan's testimony. It's good enough."

Clay's hard face softened into lines of pity. "Jake, I don't have to tell you what you already know. You're afraid of Latigo Dolan and his gunslingers. It took all your courage to ride out there with us and you haven't enough left to go again." Clay continued, speaking gently. "A fighting badge doesn't belong to you, Jake. You know it." His voice lifted with an edge of steel. "Turn the badge in, Jake. Write out your resignation."

Jake stirred. "But I—"

"If you don't, someone will tear it off your shirt. You've lost your nerve. Resign. Ride out and find a peaceful town."

Toller looked at him then at Blake and Larry. He opened the drawer and took out paper and pen.

In another moment he dropped the pen, shoved the paper at Clay. He fumbled at his badge as Clay arose, folding the resignation.

He turned to Jake. The sheriff's badge lay on the desk. Clay's voice was gentle again. "While we're gone, you can ride out, Jake. Nothing to explain that way. Good luck."

He stepped outside and closed the door. Larry looked at him, puzzled. "No sheriff, now. Where does that leave us?"

"Still with lawmen, three of 'em. We're still deputies, Larry. We represent the law, now that the sheriff has resigned." He indicated the milling group of mounted men just ahead. "That's not a mob now."

He slipped the reins of his horse from the rack and climbed into the saddle. He turned the horse from the rack and rode out, the rest of the men falling in behind.

He again rode northward to Tumbling A. This time it would be a showdown and he would lead the attack —against Lora Archer.

He suddenly wondered how important she could have been to him—had things been otherwise.

XVII

AT THE TUMBLING A ROAD, Clay held up his hand to halt the men behind him. They milled around close. His cold blue eye circled them. "This is a posse. You're under my orders, the sheriff being gone. You don't say a word or make a move without I tell you. Understand?"

They looked at one another and then at Clay. He sat ramrod straight, shoulders back, dark face harsh as the jagged mountains that cut the sky to the north. The badge glinted on his shirt and the sun caught points on the brass cartridges in the loops of the gunbelt around his narrow waist.

Randall spoke up first. "You know what you're doing, Clay. You can depend on us."

They crossed the boundary of the big ranch and each man instinctively searched the horizon. But there was no challenge and nothing moved. The large number of riders along the dusty road raised a yellow-brown plume that slowly dissipated.

They rode on, cautiously now, and Clay sent three men ahead of the main group to make sure they did not fall into a trap. Just before they reached the ranch proper, the three men came riding back. Clay halted the cavalcade.

The three reported that there was no sign of gunslingers anywhere. Clay gave brief orders that formed the men into a crude half moon and they made a slow advance. At last Clay looked down on Tumbling A. His eyes swept the buildings, the corrals and pens. There was no sign of life but Clay felt as though the place crouched and waited.

He signaled Randall and Kristan to him. "Larry, you and I will go on. Blake, you stay with the men. Hold 'em back unless something happens to Larry and me. Understand?"

Randall nodded and turned his horse. Clay loosened the gun in the holster, caught Kristan's questioning look and nodded. They slowly moved down the road to the big ranchhouse. Behind them, men waited silently. Ahead, the ranch waited just as silently.

"I'll talk," Clay said. "I'll try to get Lora Archer to parley."

"Why?"

"Could be, Larry, she's actually as innocent of these attacks as you are. Latigo could be forcing her hand."

Larry's shaggy brows lifted skeptically. "It's a hell of a wild guess."

They said no more. Silence held again. They came into the ranchyard and had advanced but a few feet toward the house when Latigo's harsh, flat voice checked them.

"That's far enough, Manning. You ain't got a chance of raiding us. We're ready for you. Turn around and ride back if you don't want a bullet."

Clay sat his horse just within the fence, facing the house. The windows had been raised from the bottom just enough to permit gun muzzles to command the yard. Clay's eyes flicked to the distant bunkhouse and, though he could see no one, he felt that it was also a fort.

His voice lifted. "This is no raid. There are three legal deputy sheriffs here. We want to speak to Lora Archer."

"She don't want to talk to you," Latigo called.

"We don't leave until we see her."

Clay waited. Kristan threw him a sidelong glance, spoke from the corner of his mouth. "Think she'll show herself?"

"If she still runs Tumbling A," Clay said cryptically.

There were more long moments of silence. Then the ranchhouse door opened, slowly. Lora appeared, turned to speak to someone inside and then stepped

148

out on the porch. She carried a rifle. Her imperious eyes rested briefly on the two riders in the yard then swept to the group waiting far behind them, came back to Clay.

Her voice was cold, demanding. "Another talk? I'm tired of listening to accusations and lies. Get off Tumbling A range."

Clay stiffened. "We came for the men who raided Ole Neff's spread. We want the men who hit the Box E."

She stared. Her cheeks flamed in anger and her hands tightly gripped the rifle. "You came *here!* You accuse *us!*"

"We do," Clay nodded.

"Then get out! None of my men have been near the Neff ranch. I don't know about the Box E. But none of my men are involved. You're blaming Tumbling A because you want an excuse to. . . . Get out!"

Clay kept his voice level. "Miss Archer, did you *ride* with the men?"

Her lips parted as the implication struck her. Latigo Dolan came up beside her. He spoke swiftly in a low voice and she shook her head, pushed him back, facing Clay again.

Clay leaned forward. "Trail sign leads right here, Miss Archer. I ask again—did you ride with your crews? Is one of your men wounded? A raider was hit at the Box E."

Latigo stepped to the rail. His hand hovered over his holster as he spoke in a cold, clipped voice. "So you snakes finally worked up enough guts to show your fangs? You heard what Miss Archer said. Rattle your hocks off Tumbling A!"

Clay didn't move. "Miss Archer, check your crew —with one of us. If there's no one missing or wounded, you have our apologies and we'll ride off. This is a serious charge—raid and murder."

Lora half turned to Latigo, his dark, handsome face set in ugly lines. His gun swept up from the holster.

"Get out!"

He fired over their heads, a warning.

The men who waited while the two parleyed, took it

as an attack. Clay heard the yell behind him and then a rifle cracked spitefully. Splinters flew from the porch eave just above Latigo's head. He whirled, grabbed Lora and slammed a hasty shot at Clay that cut so close he heard its hiss.

Clay cursed, set spurs and neck-reined his horse about, Kristan following him. Now guns roared from the house. Bullets cut about Clay as he spurred, leaning low in the saddle. His men returned the fire and guns from the bunkhouse joined in the battle.

Clay reached his men, gave swift orders that sent them racing to form a tight circle about Tumbling A. Clay sat his horse, looking at the house, the wisps of blue gunsmoke lifting from the windows.

His eyes were bleak. A general fight was a thing he had hoped to prevent, but it was done now. This would not end until one side had destroyed the other.

And Lora Archer, he thought, could stop a chance bullet as well as any of her men.

XVIII

LATIGO'S STRONG ARMS PROPELLED Lora into the house and the door slammed behind her. She heard bullets strike the wall and she stood dazed. Latigo's harsh voice directed the defense as men crouched. at the windows, returned the fire.

She caught her breath and a wave of fury swept over her. They would dare! They would trump up those ridiculous excuses to attack! She hurried toward a window, but Latigo checked her.

"Stay back, Lora. This is for keeps."

"This is my home and my ranch. I'm taking a hand!"

She wrenched free and dropped beside one of the men at the window.

Latigo watched her level a cartridge in the rifle, take aim, and then fire. A faint smile touched his lips. By God, she had spunk! His face grew solemn as he looked out the window, saw the attackers deploy about the house. Latigo had guessed wrong when he thought his bluff on Jake Toller would hold the rest of the range in check. They had almost caught him flat; only that dust cloud had been warning before they popped over the hill and descended on the ranch. Some of his men were still in the bunkhouse, so his force was split. If he could find some way of getting his men together, he'd hit those nesters hard, scatter them. A slug slammed into the heavy door even as he thought of it. No chance now with the yard bullet-swept.

Steady fire kept those within the house down below the window sills. Glass crashed as a bullet smashed

151

through a pane. Somewhere a man cursed. Lora snapped shots at occasional riders she could see at a distance. She slammed bullets at a man who tried to crawl closer to the house and saw him drop flat and scurry back. She had taught at least one man respect for the Tumbling A.

The fire slacked off. The attackers kept low and she wondered if Clay Manning planned some new devilment. She brushed a wisp of hair from her face.

There was no movement in the yard and, after the thunder of guns, the silence itself seemed to boom and echo. A man at one of the windows shifted, spoke in a low growl to his companion.

Lora paid no attention, her eyes centered on the yard. Another attack was sure to come. Clay Manning —she hated him! He had defied her father, fought Latigo, and now he headed up her enemies. She suddenly had a vivid memory of his kiss. She felt sick, and yet her mind formed an unexpected question. Would he lead such an attack without some shadow of a reason? She tried to reject the thought but it came back. She remembered what he had said, and she wondered why she had not heard of the Neffs and the Box E. Surely, Latigo or one of the hands would have known about it.

Why had he insisted that she see if one of the hands was wounded? She tossed her head. Foolish notions! As owner of the ranch, she knew all that happened. But she actually *hadn't* been with the crews. Manning had touched on something there.

She moved back from the window and came to her feet. The tense silence outside the house continued and the men around her didn't like it. Latigo came into the room, saw her and grinned.

"We're holding 'em. They'll give up after while." His face tautened. "And then, by God, they'll pay for this!"

"They should," she said shortly. Her frown deepened. "Latigo, what happened at the Lazy N? At the Box E?"

He looked at her, black eyes sharp and probing. He shrugged. "Some trouble, I guess. We're blamed for it."

"Manning said 'raids.' Had you heard of it?"

His jaw tightened. She became aware that one of the men at a nearby window listened and he watched Latigo, a peculiar expression in his eyes that she could not quite read. Latigo grunted disdainfully.

"A pack of lies, every bit of it!" He gently turned her to face him. "Lora, you don't believe him!"

"But I wasn't with the crews. . . ."

Latigo laughed. "But I was. I can tell you where every man was."

She smiled and he released her, hurrying to the rear of the house when someone called him. She felt sure again, but suddenly she wished that she could see every one of the crew for herself. She could prove then that Clay Manning was badly mistaken—if not a liar.

There was a burst of firing from the rear of the house. She hurried down the short hall and stopped just within the kitchen. Men fired rapidly out the windows, Latigo's gun among them. Then the firing stopped.

Lora asked sharply. "What's happening?"

Latigo swung around. "They made the barn."

It worried him. This drew the ring more tightly around the ranch. There was a hail from outside, repeated again. Latigo whirled and strode to the window, gun poised.

"Wait!" Lora said. "Let them talk!"

"No use," Latigo snapped. "Just gives 'em more time."

The voice was clear now. She believed it was Clay Manning. "Miss Archer! Listen to me! We can stop this!"

She spoke through a broken windowpane. "We don't give up!"

Manning's voice lifted. "We don't ask you to. We want to stop the fighting."

"Then ride off!"

"Will you give us the men who killed Ole Neff and shot Diane Epps? There'll be no lynching. I promise it. There'll be a fair trial."

Latigo cursed, stepped into the window and threw a slug at the barn. He dropped, pulling her down as return fire went through the window. It died down in a moment. Lora looked at Latigo. "Why did you do that?"

He made an angry gesture. "Manning tries to keep us busy here while they attack somewhere else. No point in falling into that trap."

"Diane Epps was shot," Lora said thoughtfully. "No wonder they're mad. But why do they blame it on us? Were some of our men over that way?"

"No!" he said sharply. "None of us were near the Box E."

She had to believe him—and yet there had been a ring of truth in Manning's voice. It bothered her more and more.

Then a fury of gunfire broke again. The attackers tried to reach the house in a storming rush. Guns thundered in the room so that Lora was deafened. A man near her screamed and fell, grabbing at his chest.

Blue smoke swirled about the room, the smell of cordite almost choking. Two men had been wounded, one of them seriously. Latigo ordered the man taken out and Lora led the way to one of the bedrooms.

He was stretched out on the bed and Lora hastily ripped open his shirt, saw the ugly bullet hole in his chest. She hurried into another room for bandages and water, returned and started to work as guns sporadically sounded outside.

She finally had him bandaged but she did not like the gray color that came in his face, the strange, ragged way in which he caught his breath, held it for a long uncertain moment and then exhaled with a weary sigh.

Latigo came in, glanced at the man on the bed. "How is he?"

"I don't know. He needs a doctor."

"A fine chance of getting one!" He nodded grimly toward the window. "Do what you can for him, Lora."

He started to leave but she checked him. "Latigo, there'll be more men shot."

He stared. "Sure—but mostly on their side." His voice sharpened in disbelief. "You don't want to throw in the fight!"

She shook her head. "Of course not, but if there was some way to stop?"

"A truce? A surrender?" he demanded. He laughed, a grating sound. "No, by God! We finally got them out in the open, all in one bunch. Think I'm going to give up now because a couple of men have been hit!" He strode out of the room.

He acts as though he owns the ranch, she thought. She shrugged it off worriedly and turned to the wounded man. He looked at her with pain-filled eyes. She hurried to his side, suddenly hopeful, but she realized that his breathing was still difficult and the pallor had not left his face. He moistened his lips and she gave him a drink of water, supporting his head.

He lay back with a sigh, spoke with difficulty. "I'm pretty hard hit, ain't I?"

"Hush," she admonished. "Don't fret. I've patched you up. We'll have a doctor here before long."

A gun exploded out in the yard and the man's eyes turned toward the sound. "You got to wait—until they're gone. Could be too late."

"No," she smoothed his pillow.

He looked up at her, gratefully. "You ain't going to leave? You'll be right here?"

She was touched. "All the time."

He closed his eyes weary beyond her comprehension. "I ain't going to last long. I can feel it. Sure good to have someone near . . . someone like you. You're a good woman."

"Sssssh! You have to save your strength!"

"For what?" he demanded and fought for breath. "To go on another raid, like the Lazy N?"

She stared, eyes wide in horrified surprise. He had raided the Neffs! Then Latigo must not have known of it!

The man spoke again. "That's what brought this on. All of us figured this would push 'em too far, but there was no telling Latigo. You do what he says and no questions." He looked at her. "Don't you be fooled by him, ma'am. He's gonna grab everything he can get. He don't care how he does it. Like he pushed your paw, until he got killed."

Lora's mouth was dry and her eyes were strained. She swallowed with difficulty, swallowed again until at last the words came, "Latigo—pushed Dad! He ordered these raids!"

The man went into a fit of coughing and blood appeared in the corner of his mouth. His breathing became fast and hoarse and she knew that he was about to die. He quieted, though his fingers picked aimlessly at the coverlet. His head moved from side to side.

Suddenly his eyes were open again, sane and clear. His voice came as a whisper. "Latigo can't do nothing more to me. You ought to know what he's like. He sent us to raid the Lazy N. We burnt it—killed Neff and another man."

"I can't—!"

The man kept on talking, though his eyes were closed. "I went to Chieftan and heard the squatters called a meeting about the Neff raid. That night, we hit Box E." His voice drifted off, became stronger. "Just like Old Dan would do it. Him and Latigo are a pair. Get it fair if you can. If you can't, burn and kill or drive off. That's what Dan tried to do with Jory Epps. He drew first but Epps—"

The voice was gone and the man stopped breathing. Lora stood frozen. The man had surely lied! But he was dying, her brain screamed in awful logic. He had *no reason to lie!*

What kind of man was her father? She shuddered, buried her face in her hands, honesty making her know the ugly, naked truth. Dan was always kind to her. He explained the things he did in a gentle way, making her believe that it was all necessary.

Now, from the lips of a dying gunhawk, she knew better. He must have been ruthless, hard. She could understand, if this were so, why people hated Tumbling A. She recalled the way people kept their distance in town and how, at dances, she and Latigo were invariably alone.

The dead man had said Latigo pushed her father on to hard, cruel acts. Looking back, she could remember when small spreads had been added to Tumbling A. She had assumed that her father purchased them. Pos-

156

sibly he had—but what pressure had been brought against the seller?

She remembered her own ultimatum to Clay Manning—sell, or else—and she realized how that must have sounded. She gave a shuddering sigh. What a fool she had been, hating, believing that her father's death had been deliberate murder.

Wrong—all wrong! She looked about the room, slowly, and her eyes rested on the silent figure on the bed. Here was blood on her hands, because of her own blind hatred and folly. Another was wounded in the kitchen. How many on the other side had died?

She could name them. Jory Epps, Ole Neff, the man with him. Diane Epps shot. Mark it up to Tumbling A and its gunhawks. How many had her father and Latigo killed before Dan had died?

Her eyes filled with tears. She dashed them away, took a deep breath, and walked out into the hall. She looked in the kitchen. Latigo was not there. The men gave her a glance and dismissed her, giving their attention to the yard.

Her voice sounded, firm and clear. "Put up your guns. We're not fighting any more."

They whirled about. One man blurted an amazed "What!"

"We're not fighting any more. I want to know who was at the Lazy N. Who was on the Box E raid?"

"Lora!" Latigo's voice boomed behind her. "What are you doing?"

He pulled her around. She gasped. "Leave me go. I'm giving orders. To stop the fight."

He propelled her into the hallway. His voice was low and harsh. "Are you crazy, Lora!" He waved toward the yard. "You know what they believe about us."

Her eyes locked with his and then she went to the bedroom door, opened it. Latigo looked in on the dead gunman then inquiringly at her.

"He told me," she confronted him. "I know what father must have done and how you helped him. I know the Tumbling A men were at the Lazy N. They were at Box E."

A slight flush touched his lean cheeks then was gone. His eyes hardened but he spoke evenly. "So, you know. And you know about Dan. Think on it, Lora. Why I did it. Dan had a dream, not only for himself but for you. I helped him try to bring it about. He couldn't, those wolves killed him. Sure, he hit them and hit them hard, but you don't fight nice in a game like this, Lora. You don't stand still."

He took a step toward her, his voice intent. "You wouldn't make a move, and we had to keep pushing. I wanted a showdown, a chance to break them once and for all. Then we take over—like Dan wanted. But the coyotes have to be whipped first. And Clay Manning heads them up."

"Why?" she asked. "Because Father tried to run him out. Because you ordered the men to beat him up when he danced with me." Her voice quavered and she edged around him. "I know who the wolves are."

"Lora, I—" He started to take her hand but she flung it away.

"Don't touch me, Latigo. I loved my father. I think I could have loved you. But neither of you told me the truth. Now that I know it was Father—and you—and the gunhawks you hired who are the real wolves of Morala Valley, do you expect me to keep this up?"

She ran down the hall to the front room. He caught up with her and the men at the windows turned.

"Lora! What are you doing!"

She was near tears as she pulled away. "I'm nearly a wolf myself. What did you and Father try to do to me! I'll have none of it. If Tumbling A burned and killed, then Tumbling A will pay the price. I'll not protect killers!"

She whirled to the door and jerked it open. She had no thought that hostile guns waited outside. She ran to the edge of the porch and heard Clay Manning's surprised shout.

She heard Latigo curse thickly behind her. She gripped the porch rail and stared out into the yard. Men cautiously lifted their heads and Manning appeared from behind a line of bushes.

She called, "It's over. I know the truth! Come get your man!"

Rough hands seized her and brought her about. She had a glimpse of Latigo's strained face as he propelled her to the door. His shove sent her stumbling inside. Then he turned and his gun roared.

XIX

LORA CAUGHT HER BALANCE, knocked up against a table, nearly tipping it over. She swung around as Latigo slammed the door. His harsh voice called a command and guns cracked from the window.

Lora sprang to the nearest man, wrenched at his weapon. "Stop it! Stop it, I tell you!"

Once more Latigo's hands grabbed her and she was pulled away. He glared at the men. "Keep fighting. If you don't they'll lynch you."

"That's not so!" Lora cried but Latigo bodily carried her to the sofa and dropped her there.

She tried to get up but he forced her back. She saw everything in a haze of panting anger as she fought with fists, feet and fingernails but Latigo's greater strength overpowered her. Tears streamed down her face.

Latigo, breathing heavily, wiped the blood from a long scratch on his cheek. "That's better, Lora. Now listen to reason."

"Reason? What reason?" she sobbed. Her head lifted in a new flash of anger. "You dare do this to me in my own house! On my own ranch!"

"Lora, listen to me," he begged.

"You've disobeyed orders. You've lied to me. You've made me responsible for every crime in the book!"

"You have to listen, Lora. It's too late to do anything else." He caught the flash of her eyes and he spoke low and fast. "Don't you understand?"

"Understand murder?" she cried.

"We didn't expect that. Lora, Dan wanted the whole Valley. He hired me to help him get it, and I hired men I knew would do the job. Then Dan died. I figured you held back because you're a woman . . . soft. So I ordered the boys to drive out the Neffs. Then I ordered 'em to hit the Box E. I figured this would scare the others and there'd be no need of gunplay. We could buy up what we wanted. They'd be afraid to argue price or stick around the Valley."

He read the disgust and loathing in her eyes and anger glinted in his own. "Don't you understand! It was done for your good."

"My good!" She studied him and then she spoke with a touch of awe. "Is that the way you explain it? Why, you're mad! You're gun crazy!"

"Is it crazy to build up the biggest ranch a man ever saw for the girl he loves and hopes to marry!"

Her eyes widened and her voice dropped to a whisper. "You *are* crazy! Father wanted me to marry you. You knew that."

"Of course I did, Lora!" He leaned toward her but she drew back, shaking her head.

"You expected to own Tumbling A. So you took control of the ranch. The men take orders from you. You've lied to me—kept me in the dark. It begins to make a strange sort of sense—like the thinking of a sidewinder."

His dark eyes glistened as his lips drew back. There was a hail from outside and one of the men called over his shoulder. "Latigo, they want to parley."

"To hell with 'em. We'll parley with lead!"

Lora jumped up. "No! Tell them we'll talk!"

The men looked from her to Latigo, who said but three words, "I give orders."

They turned to the window and one of them fired as Latigo roughly pulled Lora to a seat beside him. His smile was tight and his eyes sharp with anger and excitement. "You can't stop things now, Lora. You have to ride the trail I've marked out."

When Latigo had pulled Lora from the porch rail, Clay Manning had dropped behind the bushes just as the gunmen sent bullets whipping through the space where he had stood a few seconds before. He cautiously lifted his head and studied the house, silent now. He wondered what went on behind its blank walls.

Something had happened between Lora Archer and Latigo Dolan, Clay felt a renewed hope. She obviously wanted to surrender but Latigo had prevented her. This meant a division, and Clay wondered if it could be used to advantage.

He pushed back from the bushes, keeping low until he could work his way around the buildings to the barn. A bullet from the bunkhouse sought him out as he darted from one corral to another, but some shots from the barn discouraged the gunman.

Finally Clay made the barn. Randall, Kristan and three men held it. Clay looked toward the ranchhouse and Kristan put fresh loads in his Colt. He looked at Clay. "How you figure them?"

"I don't know exactly," Clay said. "She wanted to give up. Latigo wouldn't.

"A trick," Randall snapped.

Clay shook his head. "I figure that girl has just learned what's been happening in Morala Valley."

Randall looked at Clay, a brow raised in disbelief. "Just learned! Hell, ain't she owner of Tumbling A? She's known all along."

"I've always felt someone filled her with lies and kept her fooled—until now."

"Then why don't she turn peaceful?" Randall grunted.

"Latigo won't let her." Clay frowned at the house. "I wish I knew what was going on in there. If the crew obeys her, they'll surrender. If Latigo's the real ramrod, they'll fight."

"We're caught in a forked stick," Kristan said ruefully. "I sure wish we could end it. Three of the boys have been hit. It could be really bloody if Latigo's boys rush us."

Clay nodded grimly. "They're divided between the ranch and the bunkhouse. Helps us keep them pinned down."

162

"Most of them are there," Kristan indicated the house. "They could still play billy hell if they come out shooting."

Randall spoke impatiently. "Sounds like we're all in a bind—them and us. How you figure to end it?"

Clay spoke slowly. "Latigo could be having trouble holding the men if Lora Archer knows the truth. Just a little thing could swing things her way."

"What?" Randall demanded.

"Call for a parley. If she's in control, we'll get it."

He cautiously stepped to the door and examined the house. He glanced at Kristan then lifted his voice in a loud shout. "Hold your fire. We want to talk."

He waited. He pictured the argument that might be going on inside. He moved clear of the door, called again. Beyond the house, he saw possemen look cautiously over the edge of the bushes.

Clay called to the house again. "No point shooting one another if—"

The bullet whipped by his head. He jumped back, heard the echoes of a shot from the front of the house. He had his answer, he thought grimly. Guns sounded around him as Randall and the others returned the fire.

The guns ceased. Clay turned from the door to meet Randall's grim look. "If you're right, Latigo rules the roost in there. Me, I figure him and that witch have patched things up."

Clay grimaced. "I can't believe it, Blake."

"What now?" Kristan asked. "There's no dealing with 'em."

Clay rubbed his hand wearily along his jaw. He realized how long he had gone without rest and he had to fight off the weariness and disappointment that flooded him. He dare not let this siege go into the night. Darkness would work to Latigo's advantage. Nor did Clay know how long he could keep his posse together. They were fired now with vengeance, but they had ranches, families. Sooner or later they would want to attend to them.

He looked at the bunkhouse. "How many in there?"

Randall answered quickly. "About four, I reckon."

Clay nodded. "Just enough to cause us trouble. I'll get the boys at the front of the house. A quick rush will take care of those four if you can keep Latigo's gunhawks away from the windows in the ranchhouse."

"We can do it," Kristan nodded. "Then what?"

Clay's face grew angular and grim. "The main house —a rush from all sides."

He gave final instructions. The men in the barn would pour concentrated fire on the ranchhouse the moment Clay fired three shots in swift succession. Clay worked his way around to the front. He called all but three men from the bushes and trees and, well out of bullet range, outlined the next move. They nodded in grim approval and Clay turned to lead them into position for attack on the bunkhouse.

He saw the lone rider racing toward them and halted the men. As the rider sped closer, he recognized Lew Mahler. The man came to a sliding halt, jumped from the saddle. His freckled face was grim.

"Hank Mears just come over."

"Diane!" Clay exclaimed. "What about her?"

"She's dead," Lew said.

It hit Clay like a blow in the stomach. He half turned, eyes closed. Fury swept him that he fought to control. He dimly heard the vindictive swearing of the men and caught some of their words.

"—hang every damn one of 'em!"

"—and the woman, too! By God, she ordered that raid!"

A new fear hit Clay, jerking him around. He stared, seeing the boiling, raging anger that makes bloodthirsty animals of men. The shock of it cleared his head. "Wait! One woman's dead. Do you want to murder another?"

"But she's behind it!" a man yelled.

Clay glared. "You're still a posse. Remember that."

"How long?" someone demanded.

"Until we get back to town with the one who killed Diane Epps."

"And him in there?" Lew Mahler looked toward the besieged ranch.

"Wait," Clay said. "Lew, cover me."

164

He strode toward the house. Lew caught up with him. Clay warned him to drop to a crouch when they were just within range. They made the line of bushes without incident. Clay looked back over his shoulder, to see the posseman arguing violently among themselves. He faced the house again.

"We'll make a deal!" he called.

He waited a second and then lifted his voice again. "We want just one man. Diane Epps is dead. We want her killer. The rest of you can ride out of the Valley."

He saw movement at one of the windows. The moments dragged and he looked back at his men again. They now moved toward him. Clay faced the house again. "Just the one man! Do you fight to save a woman-killer? Are you all yellow snakes?"

The possemen crept up close to Clay. They looked at him and then at the silent house. Clay held his breath. He heard the sudden, muffled sound of a gunshot within the house.

The door flew open and a man stepped out, hands held high. The man beside Clay leveled his gun, his eyes filled with hate. Clay knocked it down, came to his feet, his gun blurring from the holster and menacing the men about him.

"I'll shoot the first man who tries gunplay. This is surrender, you fools!"

He whipped around as a shout came from the house and two more men appeared on the porch. "We ain't fighting. We're coming out!"

They stepped gingerly down into the yard. The bunkhouse door was flung wide. Four men came out, their hands also high.

"Come this way," Clay called. "Move slow and easy."

The men around Clay stirred. He spoke in a low, harsh voice. "Don't get lynch-rope ideas. I've warned you. We're not turning into hang-noose vigilantes."

Randall and Kristan appeared in the barn door, their men behind them. Randall argued but Kristan shook his head. They moved toward the bunkhouse, keeping a wary eye on the main building. More men appeared and now the crew of the Tumbling A walked

165

across the yard, hands high. Clay met the first, saw that his holster was empty. He waved the man on, eyes sweeping the rest.

Clay looked toward the house again. No one else came out. As he looked the door slammed. He turned to the nearest gunman. "Where's Latigo?—and Miss Archer?"

The man shrugged. "Latigo and us had an argument. He decided to stay."

"And Miss Archer?" Clay snapped.

The man avoided Clay's accusing eyes. "You heard a shot? Latigo wanted to keep us all fighting for him. He winged Joe over there." He pointed to a gunhawk who nursed a bloody arm. "But we had too many guns."

"Why didn't you bring Latigo?"

"It's up to the law to get its own men," the gunhawk said. "He's got Miss Archer and he figures to stay. That's your worry—not ours. None of us killed Diane Epps. Latigo did."

Clay understood, in a way, the twisted code that would not allow these men to turn Latigo over to the law even though they refused to fight for him any longer.

He turned to the house, cupped his hands around his mouth as he shouted. "Latigo! You can't win! Come out! I promise you a trial!"

XX

LORA ARCHER'S WORLD HAD CRUMBLED. When, despite her own demand to accept the parley one of the men had fired a defiant shot on Latigo's order, the echoes blasted away the last shred of myth on which her whole life had been built.

She faced it in a peculiar dull horror. Her father had been the kind Dr. Jekyll to her and a Mr. Hyde to all others. Tumbling A was a ranch to be hated and feared. There was nothing to support the pride she had felt all these years.

Once she looked at Latigo, her eyes round with wonder in an expression he could not read. He was handsome, sure of himself and she had often told herself that he was a man any girl would be proud to marry—dependable. She looked away and Latigo caught the loathing in her eyes. He was no more than one of the gunhawks, as she called them that now, instead of "hands."

But Latigo was the worst of all. He had been a willing tool for a monstrous crime against all of Morala Valley. He had made Lora herself a symbol of cold and calculated ruthlessness.

She barely heard Latigo's pleading words. "Come, Lora, think it out. What else could I do to build up this place—for you?"

Again he saw her loathing. Her lips curled. "You like burning—hurting people—killing them!"

His eyes grew mean and a muscle jumped in his jaw. His voice dripped acid. "So we're better than all the rest! We've lived on what Dan Archer did and Latigo Dolan's work but we don't want it to touch us. All right. I figured to get Manning and beat down the rest. They've split up. We'll get the bunch in the barn first and then you'll see what will happen to the others."

"No! I forbid it!"

He laughed. "You forbid it! Lora, who in hell do you think runs the ranch now? Who handled your dad? Me, Latigo. I'm still running Tumbling A!"

He called the men, gave orders that sent them out to the kitchen, except one or two who remained at the windows. Latigo forced Lora to go with him.

A man at the door turned. "About five in the barn, Latigo. We can take it easy."

Latigo nodded, pleased. He assigned two men to make a covering fire. He held Lora's arm as he talked and then he looked at her. "You and me will watch it."

A man from the front room called out. "Latigo! They're circling back your way!"

"Wait," Latigo told the men, and pulled Lora with him to the front room. He looked out the window, frowning. Lora saw Clay Manning and a bunch of men well out of gun range and then she saw the distant rider.

"Who do you reckon he is?" the man at the window asked.

Latigo shook his head, and continued to watch. Clay Manning and a man broke from the group and came toward the house, boldly at first. They dropped below the screen of bushes and Lora could not see them any more.

Latigo spoke swiftly. "They're planning something. We'll beat 'em to it."

Manning's voice lifted. Diane Epps was dead! Lora gasped. Manning offered to let the rest go if Diane's killer was turned over to the posse. Who was it? She noticed that the men eyed Latigo in a peculiar way.

Her face blanched as she turned to him. "You!"

"An accident!" he said. The response was almost automatic. Manning's voice lifted again, asking if they defended a woman-killer. The men in the room glanced at one another. Outside, Clay's voice sounded

168

again. "Yellow snakes!" he exclaimed, and one of the men flushed.

Another took a deep breath. "It's one thing to do a shoot-out, another to kill a woman. I never thought of it that way. I reckon I'll throw in my chips."

He turned and Latigo's cold voice stopped him. "You hired out for a job. You'll stay and do it."

"Sure, the usual sort of gunslinging. But now Mrs. Epps is dead. That bunch out there won't ever give up. I figure it's smart to take Manning's offer."

He went to the door but Latigo's gun whipped out and he fired from the hip. The slug creased across the man's arm, driving him against the wall. Lora screamed. Latigo realized that half a dozen guns lined on him. He stared at them, then up and around at hard faces in disbelief. One of the men spoke. "You can die mighty fast, Latigo."

"You'd turn me over to them?"

"I never turned no one over to the law. You can stay here if you want. We're giving up. They don't want us—now."

He kept his gun leveled on Latigo as he opened the door. He looked at the others. "I'll keep Latigo covered. Shuck your guns and walk out, hands high so they can see 'em."

One by one, the men edged out the door. The wounded man moved out, clutching his arm. Then the last man stepped out on the porch, still facing Latigo.

"Good luck, *hombre*. You'll need it." He dropped his gun and reached the edge of the porch in two long strides, arms high.

Lora suddenly realized she was alone with Latigo and that the door stood wide open but a few steps away. She lunged for it but Latigo's hand darted out like a striking snake. He spun her around and back so that she stumbled half across the room, falling asprawl the sofa.

He slammed the door, peered out the window, dark face a mask of hatred. Lora stirred and he swung around to her. She shrank back at the blazing, angry eyes. Her glance swept the room, saw the guns the men had dropped at the door.

Latigo grinned wolfishly. "You wouldn't have a chance."

His eyes briefly raked her. "Nor out there, either. I know what they'd do."

She was silent a moment. "But do you have to keep me here?"

He emptied the last gun, pitched it aside. He spoke harshly. "Why, they'll be careful because you're with me. They won't want to hit you. That gives me a chance."

A hail came from outside and Latigo sprang to a window, catfooted, his Colt ready in his hand. Lora heard Clay Manning's voice. "You can't win! Come out. I promise you a trial."

His attention was centered on the yard. Lora quietly arose from the sofa, edged around it. The door and the hallway were but a few steps. She threw a look at Latigo, still at the window.

His harsh voice lifted. "Come and get me!"

She moved fast. She was in the hall and racing to the kitchen. She heard Latigo's gasp and the heavy pound of his boots just behind her. She never quite reached the door.

His hands grabbed her shoulder even as her fingers reached for the knob. He cursed as he whirled her away. He stood spread-legged before the door, breathing deeply.

"Get this, Lora. There's a lot of men out there who want to stretch my neck. You're the one chance I got of getting out. If you spoil it, I'm dead anyhow." His voice tightened. "I've killed one woman, they tell me. I can kill another."

Her eyes widened in horror. "Latigo, you've gone mad!"

He considered it and smiled crookedly, something of wistfulness in the twist of the lips. "No, Lora, I made mistakes and I'm paying for them. I should have let things be after Dan died. Maybe you and me would've been married. It's a big spread as it is."

He hardly saw her. His eyes looked inward on the past. "But I picked up Dan's poison or maybe I had too much of my own. I tried for bigger stakes. I hit the

170

Neffs, the Box E and then I stopped. That was the second mistake. I should have swept the Valley from one end to the other, before they could organize. But the third mistake—I shot Mrs. Epps."

His voice filled with loathing. "I've lived with the gun. But I killed men—and in face-to-face fights. It's a horrible thing to shoot a woman. It rattled me. I pulled the men back here and now—" He made a circling movement indicating those who besieged the house.

"But, Latigo, surely they won't—"

His harsh laugh cut her short. "I've seen men hung for less. It won't happen to me."

"But you can't stay here! It's hopeless." She held out her hand, pleading. "Give up, Latigo. You'll get a trial. Clay Manning promised."

"Manning!" he spat. "I'll live to kill that man!"

He looked out the rear window, saw no one. He grabbed Lora's hand and went to the front of the house, looked out. The possemen had now gathered around the Tumbling A hands. She could not see Clay Manning though surely he was in the milling group.

Latigo spoke in a half whisper. "They're all out there—and they're counting their prisoners. By God, it's a chance!"

He hurried Lora back to the kitchen and looked out, peering beyond the barn. Some distance back he saw saddled horses, ridden by the men who had circled the buildings and had taken the barn. Latigo's eyes lighted.

He grinned at her. "I got luck." His eyes changed and his hand moved to his holster. "I can make the horses and you'll keep 'em from shooting. Only thing is, you'll hang back. You want me taken."

"Then leave me here," she said, seeing a sliver of new hope.

"I need your protection."

Something hard crashed against her head. She slumped forward, unconscious, and Latigo took her falling body over his shoulder.

He shifted her weight and then opened the door. There was no challenge from the barn. He held his gun ready as he moved quickly from the house. He kept

171

the building between himself and the possemen until he was close to the barn. Lora hung across his back, an effective shield.

He cut to the barn, covering the few yards swiftly despite Lora's weight. He darted around the far side, paused for breath. Hope was strong now as he looked toward the trees where the saddled horses waited. He would have to leave the shelter of the barn and he knew he would be seen. But the girl on his back was protection. Once in the saddle the odds for his escape mounted.

He started for the horses, keeping the barn between him and the possemen as long as he could. Then there was nothing for it but to move boldly out into the open. He had covered a short distance when he heard the shout behind him.

Clay had just given final orders to send the men in a tight ring around the house. Clay warned the men that Lora Archer was a prisoner; he had learned this from the Tumbling A hands. A sudden shout made him whirl around. Lew Mahler pointed.

Latigo Dolan was in clear sight and Clay saw the girl lying slack across his shoulders. Someone cursed.

"Get him!"

"Wait!" Clay yelled. "You'll hit the girl."

Randall cursed in turn. "He's making for the horses we left beyond the barn. He'll get away sure!"

Latigo was now close to the mounts. Clay snapped orders at Lew and Kristan. "Go after him but be careful of the girl. Let him go if you have to. I'll cut him off."

He pushed through the men and raced for the tethered horses beyond them. He picked one, vaulted into the saddle. The possemen now raced toward the barn. Far beyond, Latigo turned and fired as some of the men ventured toward him. They stopped.

Latigo reached the horses. He dropped Lora, jumped into saddle and neck-reined the horse as he fired toward the barn again. Clay saw him streak off, heading north and west.

Clay racked spurs and his animal thundered across the yard. He did not attempt to follow Latigo but rode directly west. A line of cliffs would keep Latigo from going north for several miles, forcing him west and a little south before he could plunge into the safety of the broken country.

Clay hoped fervently that Lora had not been harmed. He was thankful that Latigo had abandoned her. He raked spurs constantly and the horse stretched out in a pounding drive. He glanced at the high yellow cliffs, headed directly for the point where they made a giant's curve southward. Just beyond, there would be a hundred places where Latigo could find canyons in which to hide.

There was no sign of the man. He would be hidden by the rolling swales between Clay and the mountain cliffs. Shortly, however, Latigo must turn southward. If Clay reached this point first, then there would be showdown. If Latigo made it first, he might never face justice.

Clay's spurs dug cruelly. The ground blurred by and the yellow cliffs loomed closer. A matter of minutes now, Clay thought. The meeting was abrupt and surprising. The man in black catapulted out of a swale directly into Clay's path. Both men savagely neck-reined away from each other and their hands whipped to their holsters.

The guns roared together. Clay felt the whisper of the bullet close to his shoulder. He saw Latigo thrust backward out of the saddle and drop, his riderless horse racing on.

Clay held in his mount, gun still lifted. The black figure on the ground did not move. Clay swung out of saddle and walked toward the man. He saw the glistening darker stain on the black shirt. Latigo's body shivered and then went slack. Clay slowly replaced his Colt.

He had some trouble in getting Latigo's mount, but at last he lashed Latigo across the saddle and, mounting his own horse, headed back to the Tumbling A. When he came into the ranchyard, he saw that Kristan and Randall had turned their prisoners into an empty corral. He did not see Lora and when Kristan hurried up, he asked about her.

"In the house. Shook up bad, but not really hurt."
Kristan looked at the slack figure over the saddle of
the lead horse. "You got him."

Clay nodded and wearily dismounted. "It's over,
Larry."

Kristan turned from Latigo's body. "Dan and this
one gone, maybe we can figure on peace in the Valley." He indicated the house. "You were right about
her, Clay. She didn't really know what her dad and
Latigo were doing."

Randall hurried up. He looked at Latigo and
grinned at Clay. "Good riddance. Now, what about
them?" He indicated the prisoners.

"Hired gundogs," Clay answered. "With Dan and
Latigo gone, they don't mean much. If they're out of
the Valley by morning, we won't have any argument."

One of the gunhawks, peering through the poles of
the stout corral, called to Clay. "Friend, you can depend on this jasper being gone!"

Randall was not sure, but Clay finally convinced
him to let the prisoners saddle up and ride out. "Blake,
you and some of the boys ride along to see that they
get out of Morala. No point in wasting any more time
on them."

Clay walked to the main house. As he stepped up
on the porch, he saw the raw splintered wood left by
the bullets, the broken windows. He bleakly shook his
head when he thought what destruction greed for range
could do.

He knocked. There was no answer and he knocked
again. Waiting a moment, he opened the door and
stepped inside. The big main room was empty but bullet marks and empty cartridge cases gave mute testimony to the siege.

"Miss Archer?" he called.

There was a rustle of cloth and she appeared in the
hall doorway. Her golden-red hair was disarrayed, her
eyes swollen from weeping and he saw the faint discol-
oration under her hair just below the ear. A blow
from a gun barrel would make such a mark.

Lora bit her lip and came into the room. Clay held
his hat in his hand. "I—it's over now."

174

Her shoulders squared. "I'm glad. I only learned of what really happened today."

"Yes, I figured as much. And you tried to break with Latigo." He hesitated again. "He's dead."

She spoke in a low voice. "I guess he deserved it. I guess all of us deserve whatever happens to Tumbling A."

He studied his hat. "Why, as to that, I think things will work out. . . . Of course, we're riding the gun-hands out of the Valley. That'll leave you short-handed for a time. But two or three of us will help along until you can get a regular crew."

She stared at him. "After all Tumbling A has done —!" Words failed her.

He smiled. "Some of it happened before your time. Some of it was Latigo. Once you learned the truth, you did what you could to right it. That means a lot. I reckon none of us hold anything against you, person-ally."

She groped her way to the sofa, sat down, still star-ing at Clay. Disheveled and distraught, she was still a breathtaking woman. "I just can't believe that! People will accept me?"

"You got good neighbors, fine folks. Your dad didn't believe it and Latigo didn't care. But you live right with them and they'll live right with you. You'll soon find out."

She made a pathetic, helpless gesture. "But I'm afraid—I could never face them."

Clay studied her, dwelling on the green eyes, the lovely hair, the slender body. His eyes dropped to his hat again.

"Lot of people didn't understand what was happen-ing. Now they will. Give it a month and you'll see a big difference." His face lighted and he gave her an uncertain look. "Try meeting them in a month. There's a dance—"

"No!" she exclaimed, and then laughed nervously. "I couldn't go. Especially alone."

"I reckon that's true." Clay took courage. "But you could go with one of your neighbors."

"Who?"

"I'd be right pleased, ma'am."

She looked at him, startled. She realized that he offered to smooth the way for a new era for Tumbling A and its neighbors. None would question her if Clay Manning believed in her.

Her eyes softened. Something strange and electric passed between them. Clay felt a new lift and a new hope after all this time of tension. Her clear, steady eyes were upon him, reading him.

He looked down at his hat. "I sure hope you come to like your neighbors. I know some of them like you."

Her voice lifted, the despondency vanished. "I'm sure I—will."

Once more he looked up and their eyes met, held.